I CAN'T EVEN *THINK* STRAIGHT

DEAN ATTA

Quill Tree Books
An Imprint of HarperCollinsPublishers

Quill Tree Books is an imprint of HarperCollins Publishers.

I Can't Even Think Straight
Copyright © 2025 by Dean Atta
All rights reserved. Manufactured in Harrisonburg, VA,
United States of America.
For information address HarperCollins Children's Books, a division of
HarperCollins Publishers, 195 Broadway, New York, NY 10007.
www.epicreads.com

ISBN 978-0-06-315803-0

Typography by Jenna Stempel-Lobell
25 26 27 28 29 LBC 5 4 3 2 1
First U.S. edition, 2025

for Tom

PROLOGUE:

SUMMER HOLIDAY, LARNACA, CYPRUS

ON A SUN LOUNGER IN LARNACA

"Oh my God, they're here,"
my best friend Vass whispers in my ear.
Their long, flowing hair tickles my shoulder.
Vass's fresh application of sunblock
invades my nostrils as their pale, long, lean body
invades my personal space as usual.

"It's the last day of our holiday.
You gonna talk to Local Boy today?" I ask.
I don't look up from the book I'm reading:
Gay Club! by Simon James Green.

I don't need to look up to feel
Vass's eyes roll.
I know what they wanna say:

Don't assume their gender!

But if Local Boy isn't cis,
I don't know who is.

We've been referring to him as Local Boy
because we don't know his name.
He's tall, tanned, toned, and has six-pack abs.
He's so comfortable in his olive skin,
it's hard to look at him
without making comparisons,
so I don't look at him.

Vass does enough for the both of us.

Since Vass first saw Local Boy
on the second day of our holiday,
we've abandoned our mums
to return to this specific spot
on this specific beach every day.
I've missed out on weeks
of mum-and-son quality time.

I guess I shouldn't complain.
While Vass has been swooning,
I've done a ton of reading,
and written some poems in
my new sky-blue notebook.

My old notebooks at home
contain more poems, short stories,
and the start of a novel.
I dream of being an author,
but I've no idea how to
make that dream come true.

Mum will be reading right now, too.

She has a huge reading list for her master's degree.
Mum works full-time, studies part-time,
and has a market stall side hustle.

Mum will be at the private beach.
A treat from Theía Estélla, Vass's mum,
who is a literal angel to us.

Vass and I could be there with them,
but we're at the public beach
because Vass has a crush on Local Boy.

"Don't look now," says Vass.

"I'm not looking." I laugh.

"I want you to look,
but be discreet about it.
Check if Local Boy
is checking me out."

Vass snatches the book I'm reading
and reclines in their sun lounger
under a sun umbrella.
They pretend to read
like a spy with a newspaper.
The book is upside down.

The angel on my shoulder tells me
to tell Vass to turn the book around.
The devil on my shoulder tells me
to take a photo to tease Vass with.

My phone makes the camera shutter sound.

"Τι κάνεις? Μαλάκα!" Vass hisses.
They drop the book and grab my phone.

I lean over to watch Vass zoom in
to the background of the photo.
Local Boy is either looking directly at Vass
or directly at the camera: at me.
It's hard to tell because of the angle.

"I think this is the first time you haven't
zoomed in on yourself in a photo," I tease Vass.

"I think you're right," says Vass,
"I have to talk to them today."

"I didn't say you had to," I reply.
"I asked if you were going to.
It's fine to have a crush
without having to act on it."

Vass waves away my words
like a fly that's bothering them.
"Should I wave at them from here,
or be bold and go over there?"

A cool shadow looms large over us.
"Did you just take my photo?"

Vass and I scream, startled.
Local Boy smiles, friendly, pleased.

"Παναγία μου!" Vass laughs.
"What a way to make an entrance.
You frightened us."
Vass bats their mascaraed eyelashes
and passes my phone back to me.

I pinch the screen to zoom out,
and hold my phone up defiantly.
"I was taking a photo of my best friend
and you just happened
to be in the background."

I look around for Local Boy's minions,
but he seems to be on his own today.

"Well, I'm still in the photo,"
says Local Boy,
"so, technically I was right."

Local Boy pronounces all four syllables
of "tech-nic-cal-lee,"
as if it's his word of the day.

"Do you like being right?"
Vass flirts with Local Boy.

"I can be wrong sometimes,"
Local Boy flirts back.

I roll my eyes and tut.
I snatch my book from Vass's lap.

"I'm Vass, by the way."
Vass puts out a hand,
which Local Boy takes
and slowly shakes.
"And my pronouns are
they, them, theirs."

Local Boy eyes up
Vass's long, aurora-manicured nails,
like Vass is an exotic
sea creature washed ashore.
"Nice to meet you, Vass.
I don't think I've met
a nonbinary person before."

"There's a first time
for everything," says Vass,
stretching out on their sun lounger
like a relaxed cat.
"So, what's your name?"

The devil on my shoulder tells me
I should be angry
Vass hasn't introduced me,
but my angel tells me
this is Vass's moment.

"I'm Adonis,
and my pronouns are
he, him, his."

Adonis turns to me
with an expectant smile.
"And you are?"

For a moment I forget I'm really here,
beside my best friend,
on a sun lounger in Larnaca,
and not watching this through a screen
or reading it in a book.

The way Adonis looks
directly at me, into me,
I wonder if this could be
my moment.

"Me?" I say.

"Yes, you." Adonis laughs.
"Who are you?"

His "who" and "you" in his Cypriot accent
sound like the hoot-hoot-hooting of an owl
that echoes in my mind,
and reminds me of something I once read.

I remember it's *Skellig*,
my favorite book in primary school
and possibly my favorite book ever.

But unlike Skellig,
Adonis doesn't appear to be
any kind of angel.

BACK TO SCHOOL:

LONDON, UNITED KINGDOM

MONDAY: QUEER TALK–LUNCH HALL

I talk to Matt in the hushed tone
we always use for queer talk at school.
We're sitting at our regular table
in the lunch hall, just the two of us as usual.

"And then Adonis asked me
if he could borrow Vass."

Matt puts down his slice of pizza
and puts a hand up to his mouth,
demonstrating a silent gasp.
His bicep bulges beneath his shirt,
bigger than before summer.
"What did you say to that?"

"I said he'd be doing me a favor.
I was just trying to read in peace."

"Great response—very nonchalant.
But how did you actually feel?"

"I felt gutted. I don't know why,
but for a second I thought
Adonis might've been interested in me,
and not Vass.
And get this: when Vass came back
from being with Adonis
for the entire afternoon,
they wouldn't tell me anything
about what happened.
Don't you think that's rude?
After I'd spent my entire holiday
keeping Vass company
while they pined after that boy."

"They didn't tell you anything?"

"Zip, zilch, nada.
When I started asking questions,
they said to get my own love life
and keep out of theirs."

"Maybe they're right."

"Excuse me? Why are you siding with
someone you've never even met?"

"I'm always on your side, Kai.
But you read all those love stories,
and all that soppy poetry,
and yet you only tell me
about Vass's crushes,
and never your own.

From what you've told me—
and I can only go by
what you've told me,
because, as you've rightly pointed out,
I've never met Vass—
but from what you've told me,
Vass makes it obvious
when they like someone."

"So, what you saying now?
You'd be fine with me
crushing on boys at school?
Are you ready for me to come out?"

"You know where I stand, Kai,
I told you before summer:
I don't plan to come out at high school,
like in those Heartstopper books
you love so much, but
you do you."

You do you.
I hate this expression with a passion.
What does it even mean?

My eyes drift to a poster
on the wall behind Matt:
an upcoming author talk and a book signing.
I'm excited by the idea
of meeting someone who writes for a living.
I have so many questions.

Then Matt asks me,
"Don't you think it's odd
your two best friends haven't met?"

Matt wants to hook up with Vass,
says the devil on my shoulder.

I've never told Matt
about the devil on my shoulder
because I worry
that he'll think I'm crazy
or maybe even evil.

I force a smile and explain to Matt
for the umpteenth time:
"You're a school friend.
Vass is a family friend.
Vass and I are like cousins.
What's odd about that?
You haven't introduced me
to any of your cousins."

"I just thought it could be a laugh,"
says Matt, in a fake-casual voice,
"if the three of us hung out sometime.
I don't have any other queer friends,
and you've got two. So . . . ?"

Tell him about himself, says my devil.

"You don't have any other queer friends,"
I say forcefully, through gritted teeth,

"because you're afraid to come out.
And I didn't come out before summer
because you begged me not to.
You're trying to rewrite history now
with this 'you do you' nonsense,
but that's not what you said before summer."

I feel much better after this controlled explosion.
I won't stand for Matt's attempts to gaslight me.

Matt scrunches his right hand
into a fist in front of his face
and bites it in frustration.
"I didn't beg you not to come out."
His whisper is quieter than before.
"I said I was worried
it would draw attention to me,
as your best friend,
or should I say, your best *school* friend,
if you were to come out."

"Exactly! It was emotional blackmail.
You kept me in the closet with you.
You know that wasn't fair of you?"

He's ashamed of you, says my devil.

He's ashamed of himself, says my angel.

Matt looks over his shoulder toward
Nathan Anderson and The Boys:
a group of Black boys in our year.

"Just eat your pizza, Kai.
You know how you get when you're hungry."

I take a small bite of my BBQ chicken pizza
followed by a much bigger bite.
Matt's right: I'm hungry.

Matt continues to speak as I eat.

"Let's not argue in the lunch hall anymore.
Let's leave these silly arguments in the past.
Our whisper arguments are the kinda thing
that'll have people asking if we're a couple."

Matt says "couple"
as if it's the worst thing imaginable,
as if us being a couple
would ruin our final years of school,
would cast a shadow across
the bright path to his straight-passing future,
would bring shame on his religious family,
and see him cast out for shame,
as if being perceived
to be in a couple with me
is a threat to everything
that matters to Matt.

He weighs his words before he speaks again.

"Don't take this the wrong way, Kai.
I'm not being rude,

but your cane rows look busted."

Matt's short afro is always neat.
He keeps an afro comb
in his back right pocket.
It has a black, fist-shaped handle
and long, narrow metal tines.

"I know." I swallow
my final mouthful of pizza crust,
my face hot with embarrassment.
"My mum didn't have time
to redo them last night,
but I'm gonna ask my granny
to do it today after school."

READY OR NOT?–AFTER SCHOOL–
GRANNY'S KITCHEN

My sixteen-year-old cousin T
breathes deeply
                        opposite me
                        at the kitchen table.

Silence has descended on
our previously heated conversation.

The heavy smell of curried goat
has fully settled into my clothes.
The still-hot pots sit on the stove
waiting for Granny to plate up
when she returns from picking up
Olivia and Sophia, my five-year-old
identical twin cousins, from school,
as she does every weekday.

T stands and towers over me.
He can only achieve this because I stay seated.
We're the same height standing up,
but, right now, I feel stuck to my seat.

T has been bubbling and spilling over
for the past twenty minutes,
but now he's softly simmering.

T's deep voice is softer than before:
"What I don't understand, cuz,
is why Jyoti said it so casually,
like it was common knowledge,
like she assumed I already knew."

T imitates the voice of Jyoti,
a gossipy girl in my year
who T's been dating since summer:
"'Kai and Matt must miss each other,
being apart all summer.
They're so cute together.'"

T sucks his teeth.

He returns to his own voice:
"What does Jyoti have to gain
by saying you're being 'cute' with a next man?"

I wanna tell T:
Jyoti's speculation might come from the fact
that she used to fancy Matt.
I wanna get T off my back,
but I don't want him to feel bad about himself
thinking he's only Jyoti's second choice.

If T had simply asked if I was gay,

I'm pretty sure I would've said yes,
but because this involves Matt,
it feels more complicated than that,
more complicated than it should.

I'm angry at Jyoti for gossiping,
but that's kinda her whole thing.
I'm angrier at Matt
for putting me in a position
where I feel forced to lie to my cousin.
T is a year older than me
and we're at different schools.
T is often suspended from his.

"Well, for the millionth time,
I'm telling you Jyoti's lying.
So, who you gonna believe,
your cousin or some girl you met in the park
and you've only known for six weeks?
I've been at school with Jyoti for years,
and all she does is chat nonsense."

I feel bad for calling Jyoti "some girl"
because it sounds kinda dismissive,
but I'm trying to speak T's language.

T closes his eyes, tilts his head back,
and pinches the bridge of his nose.
T breathes in deeply and out again.
T does this when he's about to punch someone:
sometimes justifiably,
sometimes just for fun.

I refuse to believe T would punch me.
The Devil himself couldn't convince me
T doesn't love me.
T would love me no matter what.

When T looks at me again, he's smiling.
"Fine, cuz. If you say Jyoti's lying, she's lying."

I look for malice in his smile,
I listen for another meaning in what he's saying,
but I see and hear only love:
love that defies logic, the love of family.
I knew he would choose to believe me over Jyoti.

I hear Granny's keys in the front door,
the sound of Olivia and Sophia
bounding over the threshold,
the Velcro of their school shoes,
the patter of their frilly-socked feet
running toward the kitchen.

Their afro puffs zoom into the room.
"Tee! Tee! Tee!" they chant in unison.

They see T first,
as my dining chair is behind
the open kitchen door.
T scoops them up into a hug,
but they wriggle to get free of T
as soon as they see me.

"Kai!" "I want Kai!" "Put me down!"

In seconds, they're wrapped around my legs.
I bend to pick them up:
"Hello there, my favorite girls
in the whole wide universe."

"It's world, not universe," they say on cue.

"Universe. Multiverse.
You are in every verse," I reply.
My special greeting for The Twins.
I kiss them each on their cheeks,
and I'm tickled by their giggles.
They kiss me back, one on each cheek.
"What game shall we play today?"
I ask as I put them down.

"Hide-and-seek!" they happy-shriek.

I cover my eyes with my hands,
and start to count:

"One . . .
          two . . .
                    three . . ."

The giggling twins run into the hallway.

                    "Four . . ."

"Mind you nah knock me over,"

says Granny as Olivia and Sophia scurry past her.

"Sorry, Granny," they say as they scramble up the stairs.

"Five . . .
    six . . .
        seven . . ."

"Come now, Malachi, let me see you."
Granny enters the kitchen, laughing.

I uncover my eyes and cease counting.

Granny's smile turns to a frown.
"You get so dark on holiday," she says.

T laughs because we go through this every year
when I return from Cyprus.
T mouths the words behind Granny's back,
imitating her gestures and mannerisms.

"You nah wear sunblock, child?" Granny asks.
"You know you half white, you can still burn.
And you aff to be careful about skin cancer.
Anyone can get it. You see?" Granny points
to a scar on her nose and behind her T copies.
"The doctor removed my mole at the hospital."

I fail to suppress my laughter,
but I'm not laughing at Granny:
I'm laughing at T's impression of her.

"Kai!" "Kai!"
I hear The Twins call from upstairs.
"Come find us!"
"Come find us!"

Blessed salvation
from my two little angels.

Granny kisses her teeth, then says:
"And tek out your cane rows after dinner."
Granny turns and talks to her pots:
"I can't believe im mother let im
go to school wid im hair like dat."

T points and laughs at me.
My cheeks burn
with angry embarrassment.
I don't like when
Granny bad-mouths Mum.
But Granny's not wrong.
Mum knows how to do my hair,
but she never makes the time.
Mum relies on Granny to do it.
Mum said there was no point
of her doing it in Cyprus
because I was at the beach
with Vass every day.
And when we got back home,
Mum went back to work
and seemed to forget
I needed my hair redone
to go back to school.

"Kai!" "Kai!" The Twins call again.

"Eight, nine, ten!
Ready or not, here I come!"
I kiss Granny as I pass her,
I pat T on his shoulder,
and run to find The Twins.

Granny hollers after me:
"When you find dem,
mek dem wash dem hands,
and bring dem come eat."

"Yes, Granny," I reply, already
mounting the stairs.

"And, Malachi," Granny hollers again.

I pause on the stairs.

"Yes, Granny?" A question this time.

No answer.

"Yes, Granny?" I call my question again.

Still no answer.

I make my way back down the stairs
and round the open kitchen door.

"Yes, Granny?" I say for a third time.

When she smiles, I catch a flash of her gold tooth.
"Welcome back, baby."
She opens her arms wide to invite me into a hug.

TUESDAY: SELF-PRESERVATION–
LUNCH HALL

I tease Matt and poke his bicep:
"Why are your arms so big?
Have you been weight lifting?"

"Yeah, I have," Matt says coyly,
"and I went to boxing boot camp over summer.
I wanna be able to defend myself,
or defend you if I have to."

I find this sweet and scary.
I deflect with a joke: "Chekhov's guns!"

"What's that mean?"

"Don't you remember
from drama class before summer?
If there's a gun early in a story,
it has to be used later.
So, now you know how to box
you'll be forced to use

your new muscles and skills
to punch someone."

Matt shakes his head at me:
"You think 'all the world's a stage' or whatever.
I don't think real life follows the rules of theater
or the rules of books and films either.
You read and watch so many stories
that you've forgotten about real life.
Real life is messy, it doesn't always make sense.
Real life isn't a story with symmetry
and a satisfactory ending."

"Then why do you let the Bible dictate your life?
Isn't the Bible a bunch of stories?"

"The Bible doesn't dictate my life, Kai.
What dictates my life is the fact
that my parents are homophobic,
and I wanna keep a roof over my head.
I just wanna do my homework
and study for my exams,
so I can go to a faraway university.
This isn't self-denial.
It's self-preservation.
I know who I am, I know I'm gay,
but I know my parents.
Maybe I'll come out at university.
We'll have to wait and see
how my *story* unfolds."

I hate the sarcastic way Matt says "story":

it's like he's mocking
everything he knows about me.

"That's all well and good for you
but what about me?"

"I've already said
you can come out if you want,
but just keep me out of it.
And if anyone asks if I'm gay, too,
please tell them I'm not.
I'll get a girlfriend if I have to."

I'm surprised by the lengths
Matt seems willing to go to
to conceal his sexuality.
He'd disobey his parents in one way
in order not to disappoint them in another.
It seems extreme to me,
but I've not lived in his house,
I've only been a guest.

I went to Matt's church once,
the pastor seemed friendly,
but Matt didn't invite me back.

It doesn't bother me anyway,
because now I work Sundays
on Mum's market stall.

"You wouldn't really
get a girlfriend?" I venture.

"You know your parents
wouldn't like that either.
And you know it
won't be fair to the girl."

"How's it fair to me," says Matt,
"for you to draw attention to us?"

Despite everything that frustrates me
about this situation,
despite the back-and-forth with Matt
about me coming out,
when Matt says "us," I allow myself
to imagine it for a moment.

I see us as a couple, here at school.
I see us the way others see us.

"Cute together," Jyoti said to T.

Matt continues:
"The moment you come out,
they'll wonder about me.".

I know Matt's emotional
blackmail isn't okay,
but I also know he's afraid,
and I also know he's right.

I decide it's best not to tell Matt
about what Jyoti said to T.
My angel and devil both agree.

We are cute together,
at school and out of school.
We would make a cute couple.

If Matt were willing to come out,
I would consider him
as a potential boyfriend.

Of course I find Matt attractive,
and when we're not arguing,
I love his company.

But I don't want a boyfriend
who plans to stay in the closet until university:
that could never be my story.

I recall my advice to Vass:
                It's fine to have a crush
                without having to act on it.

I have a crush on Matt,
                I can admit that,
but I deserve to be with someone
who'll be proud to be with me.

I allow a few more moments
of silence between us,
before I weave a new thread
into our conversation.
"Were there any hot guys
at this boxing boot camp?"

A shadow falls over Matt's face.
"Nathan Anderson and The Boys were there."

I don't catch Matt's meaning.
"Do you fancy Nathan Anderson?"

Matt shakes his head
and narrows his eyes,
like he's disappointed
I can't read his mind.

"No," Matt says. He tuts and sighs.
"Because Nathan and The Boys were there,
it was like there was no fresh air.
Someone must've told our coach, TJ,
that we all go to the same school.
TJ kept putting me with one of them.
He probably thought he was doing us a favor.
There were loads of other boys there,
but I didn't get to know anyone new."

"So, no summer crushes?" I ask too cheerily.

"Nada," Matt says flatly.

It's like Matt's shadow grows
and settles over us both.

Jyoti is standing over us.
"Sorry to interrupt," she whispers,
holding up her hands.

I notice faded henna on her palms.
"I just want to apologize—"

"Not now, Jyoti." I try to stop her
but she's on a roll.

"I didn't say you were together.
I said you looked cute together,
and I didn't say you were gay,
but I get how it came across that way.
Anyway, I thought you should know,
T said he can't see me anymore,
and I get that he has to stand up
for you, as his cousin,
but I think he's overreacting."

Matt glares at me with a WTF expression.
He understands what's happened.
Jyoti spelled it out, and Matt's a bright boy:
Matt's my favorite boy.

"Who else have you
been saying this to?" whispers Matt.

"No one," says Jyoti, her voice a pitch higher.

She's a liar! says my devil.

She's harmless, says my angel.

I look at Matt and somehow
we both know that we need to change tack,

and we become a double act.

"Jyoti, I'm sorry T stopped
seeing you because of me," I say.

But it serves you right,
my devil dares me to add.

But my angel reminds me
to keep it light and breezy,
to stay on track for the sake of Matt.

"Thank you." Jyoti puts a hand to her heart,
and I can't tell if she's being serious or not.

"Jyoti, can you do me a favor, please?"
Matt bats his eyelashes at Jyoti.

"Of course." Jyoti slow-nods dreamily.

"This isn't an accusation,"
Matt begins, "but if there's anyone else who . . ."
Matt pauses, looks at me.

I offer: "Might've got
the wrong impression?"

Matt repeats: "If there's anyone else
who might've got the wrong impression,
can you tell them we're not together
and neither of us is gay?"

My heart sinks, and Jyoti sees it.

She smiles sympathetically.

"Okay, I can do that," says Jyoti.
Her agreement reveals her gossip about us
has already spread far and wide.

PARANOIA–AFTER SCHOOL–YIAYIA AND BAPOU'S GARDEN

"Why are you friends with this Matt guy?
Not only is he a closet case,
but he's also a master manipulator.
That's a toxic combination."
Vass takes my hand
and asks with mock-sincerity,
"You're not in love with him, are you?"

Vass wears a lime-green Charli XCX T-shirt,
the word "brat" in black lowercase letters across their
chest.
It's cropped to expose their midriff.

I pull my hand away
because Yiayia and Bapou are just there
in their garden chairs by the back door,
while Vass and I sit on a swing set
we're far too big for
at the far end of the garden.

Yiayia and Bapou watch on
like they don't quite understand us,
but they're happy to provide for us, nonetheless.
Like we're winged visitors at a bird feeder:
a different species from them.

When we were little, we swung high
and it felt like I could fly.

Vass's hair was long, even back then,
and they loved it when
they were mistaken for a girl.

Sometimes we'd hold hands,
and Vass would pretend
to be my girlfriend.

Pulling my hand away just now
wasn't intended to be cruel.
It felt involuntary,
like Matt's paranoia
has rubbed off on me.

Growing up together,
Vass has always been tactile with me.
Yiayia and Bapou
never comment on it.
Neither does Mum nor Theía Estélla.
It's never felt like a problem
for me, until recently.

"Οχι, I'm not in love with Matt,

but I don't wanna ruin his life:
if his parents' reaction would be
even half as bad as he says,
I wouldn't want that on my conscience."
I stand and turn to face Vass,
the most out and proud person I know.
"I was just so inspired by you
and how you came out at school."

"I know, αγάπη μου,
but you know it hasn't been easy for me.
It's different for you;
you're not coming out as nonbinary.
You wouldn't believe
how many people still misgender me.
People who claim to be allies
don't even seem to try,
like there's no 'T' in LGBTQ+."

"You should move to my school,"
I say, half joking, half wishing.

"I bet you'd get sick of me
if we were at the same school."

"I mean, I'm pretty sick of you already,"
I tease, feeling more at ease with Vass.

They laugh.

So, tentatively, I venture my question:
"Have you kept in touch with Adonis?"

Vass waves my question away:
"Μαλάκα! Forget about him.
It was a holiday fling.
Why would I keep in touch with him?"

I think of all the possibilities
with photos and video calls.
I've zoomed in on the photo of Adonis
on several occasions at night.

"Don't answer that," says Vass.
"It's a rhetorical question."

As Vass begins to swing,
I have to jump aside
to avoid their javelin-long legs.

WEDNESDAY: THE BOYS–LUNCH HALL

"Matt's a beast at boxing," says Nathan.

"Yeah, man." Kwesi joins in.
"I was scared when TJ paired me with him."

Kwesi is Nathan's right-hand man.

The rest of The Boys,
Kojo, Abdi, and Sam, are TV canned laughter
played on Nathan's cue.

They reach across their lunch table
or around each other to fist-bump Matt
or pat him on the back.

Matt smiles with fake modesty,
loving this attention.
He said he got no air with them,
but they're really gassing him up.

This is the right kind of attention,

I imagine Matt thinking.

I can't tell if Matt's brought me
to sit with them
to quell the speculation
about our sexuality
or to show off
his newfound popularity.

We've never sat with
Nathan and The Boys
at lunch before today.

None of them have ever
spoken to me outside class.
I've kept out of their way,
and they've let me be.

Matt's summer of boxing
has changed everything.
They seem to respect him,
and so, I guess they have to
tolerate me, his best friend.

Matt and I come as a pair.

"You gonna come boxing with us
sometime, Kai?" Kwesi asks me.

I feel like Kwesi's been watching me closely.
Like I'm a question he can't answer.
Like I'm a word he can't remember.

We're in several classes together,
but this is the first time
he's chosen to speak to me.
We've been paired together in Spanish
but that was Señorita Correa's choice,
not ours.

"*No, gracias,*" I reply.
"*Estoy bien.*" I wave away
the invitation to boxing
with a flick of the wrist.
"I have no desire to be punched," I say.
"I'd like to avoid head injuries
until after GCSEs and A levels."

A pause.

I don't care how these boys see me,
but I avoid eye contact with Matt:
I refuse to act straight for his benefit.
I'm determined to be myself,
whether The Boys like it or not,
whether Matt likes it or not.
I can only act straight
when I concentrate on it.
The rest of the time, I'm pretty camp,
and a bit of a clown.

Cue more canned laughter
from The Boys.

"You're a joker, Kai," says Nathan.

"Especially in drama.
You could be a professional actor."

"I don't know about that," I say.
"I'd rather write than act.

"Matt's a better actor than me,"
my devil makes me add.

I look at Matt to see if
he catches my meaning,
but he avoids my gaze.

I'm not being fair to him.
Matt doesn't act straight;
he's just typically straight-acting,
like the rest of The Boys.

If Nathan likes me, the rest of The Boys
don't have a choice but to accept me
because Nathan is their leader
and they are Nathan's minions.

My eyes settle on Kwesi,
who is still watching me.
What's he thinking?

"You could write a boxing film.
Matt could be your leading man."
Kwesi says this like he knows something,
or more like he wants to know something.

Nathan jumps in:
"The next Michael B. Jordan."

The *Creed* film franchise
and Matt's boxing prowess
are the topics of conversation
for the rest of lunch.

In the space of a single summer,
Matt has become
                one of The Boys,
and Kwesi has become
                one to watch.

Does Kwesi know I'm gay?

Is he gay, too?

Why is Kwesi watching me?

THE FAVORITE—AFTER SCHOOL—GRANNY'S KITCHEN

Granny gives me two pieces of chicken
with my rice and peas and plantain.

"Excuse me, Granny,"
says T indignantly,
"why do I only have
one small piece?
You don't have to
make it so obvious
Kai's your favorite grandson."

Granny laughs
with a flash of her gold tooth.
"You know im vegan mother
don't feed im properly.
You get my food daily,
but I don't see Malachi
as much as you.
I muss feed im up
as much as possible."

"Nah, I don't care,
it's not fair," says T.
"The Twins prefer him to me
because you get so excited
when Kai comes round,
and The Twins copy you."

Olivia and Sophia are out of earshot
in the living room,
watching cartoons
with their food on trays on the floor.
T has always been
in competition with me,
but this is the first time
he's brought The Twins into it.

"You're soft on Kai:
you give him extra food
and extra money and
you never tell him off."

"Tell im off for what?" asks Granny.

T sucks his teeth.

Granny continues:
"And if I'm soft on Malachi,
it's because he doesn't vex me like you.
Malachi's never had police
knock pon my door for im.
You know what

the people dem round here
call you? T for Trouble."

I should keep my mouth shut now,
but I feel compelled to correct T:
"Granny doesn't give me money."

"Granny paid for you
to go to Cyprus this summer."

This is news to me.
I look at Granny quizzically.

"Hush now, Tafari.
Mind your business."
Granny laughs again
but her gold tooth
and bombastic side-eye
flash a warning at T.

I know Yiayia and Bapou
help Mum financially,
but I had no idea
Mum took money from Granny.
I feel a surge of anger at my dad,
who doesn't help Mum,
and has next to nothing to do
                              with me.

My rage rises,
but I do my best
to suppress it.

My devil tells me to throw
my plate across the kitchen,
turn over the table, and
storm out of the house.

My angel reminds me
The Twins are here,
and my dad's neglect
isn't Granny's fault.

Granny is worth more
than a million dads.

My anger turns to tears
that silently spill and slick my cheeks.

T scrunches his face,
confused or disgusted by me.
Or both.

Granny rips off
a square of paper towel
and hands it to me:
"Hush now, baby."

"You juss too wicked, Tafari,"
Granny laughs, her golden laugh,
as she lightly raps T on his head.
"You made your cousin cry."

"They're happy tears," I lie.

"They're tears of gratitude,"
I say as I wipe them away.

I scrunch the wet tissue
and toss it at T's chest.
It drops onto his lap.
He looks down at it
and back up at me.

T shakes his head,
confused or amused by me.
Or both.

I stand and hug Granny.
"Thank you for paying for my holiday,"
I sniffle into her soft shoulder.

THURSDAY: THE FEDS–LUNCHTIME–
OUTSIDE SCHOOL

Only sixth-formers
are allowed out at lunchtime,
but Matt wanted to go
along with The Boys,
and I agreed because
I'm trying to figure out
if I'm into Kwesi,
and if Kwesi is into me.

On our way back to school
from the local shops,
I see two police officers approaching us.

"Feds," whispers Abdi.

"Don't be bait," says Kwesi.

I'm tucked in the middle of the group.
The Boys are my bodyguards:
Nathan and Kojo are up front,

Matt and Kwesi are either side of me.
Abdi and Sam are at the back.

"Are you okay there?"
The white police officer speaks
directly to me somehow,
as if ignoring Nathan and Kojo.

"Me?" I ask, confused.

"Are these boys bothering you?"

I'm stunned to silence.

I'm the bait one.

This is happening because of me.

Nathan jumps to conclusions:
"You see one mixed-race boy
and six Black boys, and you think
the six of us are mugging him?"

The South Asian officer seems
familiar with Nathan:
"Firstly, this is not about race,
so you can get that particular chip
off your shoulder right now.
Secondly, this is not the first time
we've caught you out of school
when you're not supposed to be.
I'm pretty sure seven of you

aren't coming from the dentist.
That was your excuse last time,
wasn't it, Nathan Anderson?"

Nathan looks at the ground.

"Allow us, man," says Sam.
"We're on our way back to school."

"One of you can go back to school
and bring a teacher out here," says the white officer.
"The rest of you will wait with us."

The South Asian officer turns to his colleague,
perhaps with a stern or pleading look
because the white officer takes a step back.

The Asian officer turns to me.
He pulls out his notepad and pen.
"You. What's your name, please?"

I search for my voice and find it:
"Malachi," I say, trying not to cry.

He asks for my surname
and date of birth,
which I tell him.

He sends me back to school,
while he takes names and dates of birth
from the rest of the group:
a group I stand out from like a sore thumb.

As I start on my way, I hear Nathan say,
"Why are you asking for my name, bro?
You just said it thirty seconds ago."

"I'm not your 'bro,'" says the South Asian officer.

"Ain't that the truth," says Sam.

DETENTION—AFTER SCHOOL—MR. NDOUR'S CLASSROOM

Our deputy head teacher, Ms. Sarpong,
has a Progress Pride flag badge
pinned to her staff lanyard.
Our head of year, Mr. Ndour, does not.

"You're not being punished because of the police,"
says Mr. Ndour, at the front of the classroom.
"There'll be no action taken by the police.
This is entirely separate to that."

"How is it, though?" asks Kojo.

"Yeah? How is it, sir?" asks Abdi.
"The feds are the reason we're here."

"Sir has already made it clear," says Ms. Sarpong,
"that this detention is because you snuck
out of school at lunchtime without permission.
You're not here because of who caught you.
You are here as a direct result of your actions:

the choice you made to ignore school rules."

"But how is it the job of the feds
to enforce school rules?" asks Sam.

"You know as well as I do," says Mr. Ndour,
"there are other young people in this local area,
who don't attend school,
and who regularly have run-ins with the police.
Those officers keep an eye out for our students
to stop you getting caught up in all that."

Nathan mumbles under his breath:
"You say 'all that' like you're not talking about
our friends, family, and neighbors."

"What was that, Mr. Anderson?"
Ms. Sarpong asks Nathan.
She sounds like the bad guy in *The Matrix*.

"Forget it, miss," Nathan mumbles again.

"I hope you know I'm here to listen.
This could've been just Mr. Ndour
supervising a silent detention, as usual,
but I chose to free up my time
and be here to hear your points of view."

"You really wanna know
my point of view, miss?"

We all turn to face Nathan.

"Yes. I want to hear from everyone,
but if you want to get us started,
please go ahead."

Nathan lists the times
he's been stopped by the police,
with The Boys and on his own,
and then he shares this:

"And this one time when
I took my little brother to the park."
Nathan looks at me. "He's mixed race,
and he's my half brother—
we have different mums—
the police stopped us.
They said gangs were recruiting
boys as young as him
and they needed to verify
our relationship.
Not only were they insinuating
that I was a gang recruiter,
they were also insinuating
that my brother wasn't my brother.
When I called his white mum
to come chat to them,
the feds were so different with her;
they were apologizing
for the inconvenience,
but they were apologizing to her,
not me or my brother."

Kwesi, Kojo, Abdi, and Sam speak
about similar experiences
of police stops and racial profiling,
but Matt and I say nothing.

There's one minute left of detention
when Ms. Sarpong calls this sharing to a close.

"I know you may have more to say,
but I don't want to keep you
for longer than your detention time.
I can't respond to each
incident you've mentioned
but what I'll say is this:
your feelings about these
incidents are valid.
It's not fair that you've been
made to feel this way.
My door is open
if you want to discuss
any of this further
and, as your head of year,
so is Mr. Ndour's.
He and I will go away
and think about
what we can do
to better support you
because, hearing your stories,
I'm sure there are many more
students at this school
who feel the way you do
but haven't had

the opportunity to tell us."

Ms. Sarpong points up in the air,
like a cartoon lightbulb has come on:
"This would be completely voluntary—
it's not another detention by any means—
but perhaps we could meet again,
one lunchtime next week,
to carry on this conversation?"

The Boys let her question linger,
before Nathan says, "Sure, miss."
The other four shrug and say,
"Yeah." "Okay." "I guess so." "Which day?"

Matt and I say nothing.

"Mr. Ndour and I will check our calendars,
and we'll get word to you
through your form tutors."

"Great," says Mr. Ndour, who knows
Ms. Sarpong is creating extra work for him.
"You can go now, boys."

"Matthew and Malachi," says Ms. Sarpong,
"if you could stay behind for a moment."

The Boys pile out of the classroom door
and into the corridor.
They don't look back or say goodbye.

Ms. Sarpong adjusts her lanyard
and straightens the Progress Pride flag badge.
She addresses us in a hushed tone,
as if bringing us into her confidence:
"Matthew. Malachi.
Quite frankly, I'm surprised.
This isn't like you.
I didn't have you pegged as
school absconders."

She pauses, but Matt and I say nothing.

"I know we had a lot
of big personalities in the room today,
and only a limited amount of time,
but I noticed
neither of you said anything."

She pauses, again, but we still say nothing.

"Well, as I said,
my and Mr. Ndour's doors are open
if either of you want to talk
about anything."

AFTER DETENTION–THE CORRIDOR

A question is forming
as Matt and I step into
the empty corridor.

We walk in silence, side by side.

The soles of his shoes squeak,
as Matt drags his feet.

This corridor has been cleaned
during our detention:
the detritus of the day,
and the smell of sweat,
swept and mopped away,
replaced by a sparkle
and a clinical smell.

When I'm sure we're out
of earshot of Ms. Sarpong
and Mr. Ndour, back in the classroom,
I turn to Matt:

"Don't you think maybe
Nathan was projecting his feelings
about looking different to his brother
onto that experience
he had with the police,
and maybe he was projecting
his feelings about me
looking different to all of you
onto what happened today?"

"That's your takeaway from today?"
asks Matt, without waiting for my answer.
"Wouldn't you agree
mixed-race people are treated differently?"

"Yes, we're treated differently," I say,
"but I felt like today might've been
about something other than skin color."

"What was today about, then?"

"Remember when you said
you were ninety-nine percent sure I was gay,
even before I told you?"

"What's that gotta do with this?"
Matt doesn't look at me as he asks.

"I had no idea you were gay
until you told me,
but I think people can see it
when they look at me.

I think it's in the way I walk,
how I talk, my whole vibe.
It's not something I can hide."

"What you trying to say?"

"Just that I'm camp, aren't I?
I think that's another reason
I stand out from you and The Boys."

"So, you think the police thought
we were bullying you for being gay?"

"Maybe. I don't know.
I think Nathan thought it was about
me being mixed race
because of his experience with his brother.
It could've been more than one thing.
It could've been both.
It could've been something else.
Maybe I'm overthinking it."

"Yeah, maybe you are a bit," Matt says.
"But I see what you're saying," he adds.
But he's in a world of his own.

"What's wrong, Matt?"

"I'm just thinking about
what Ms. Sarpong was saying.
She was trying to get us
to come out to her, wasn't she?"

"Definitely!
When she adjusted
her little badge,
it was giving:
'Don't worry! I'm an ally.'"
I pause to think.
"Or maybe she's queer . . ."

"Do you think so?"

"I don't know."

I don't wanna say
what I'm thinking.
I don't wanna make
Matt more paranoid.
But he says it.

"Do you think the rumor
about us being together
has spread to the teachers
as well as the students?"

I let out a long sigh
in place of an answer.

I turn my head to Matt,
but he stares straight ahead
and we walk this long corridor
side by side, in silence.

"This is a nightmare, Kai."
He finally looks at me
with tears welling in his eyes.

I wanna hug him, but I know
even though this corridor is empty,
Matt will pull away from me.

"This isn't such a big deal, Matt.
There are four
out and proud
queer people in our year."

"It's different for them," Matt sneers.

"Why?" I ask, but I know.

"Because they're white,
like your precious Nick and Charlie."

There it is. It's clear to me
Matt and I see the world differently.

We may even be in parallel worlds.

We may walk side by side,
but I can't walk in Matt's shoes
and he can't walk in mine.

FRIDAY: BOYFRIENDS–LUNCH HALL

It's fish and chips Friday
in our school cafeteria:
the batter here is even better
than my local chip shop.

"You two are boyfriends, right?"
Nathan asks me and Matt
in front of the rest of The Boys.

"No," I say instantly.

"No," Matt echoes me.

"But you're both gay, aren't you?"
Kwesi's voice is gentle,
with a hint of confusion.
This isn't an accusation,
he seems to know, but
he's seeking confirmation.

Kwesi's eyes search mine

as if to say, *It's okay.*

Does Kwesi wanna know if I'm gay
because he's into me?

I wanna say yes but I know Matt
isn't ready to come out.

Nathan jumps in:
"It's okay if you are gay,
bisexual, pansexual,
queer, or whatever.
My sister's a lesbian."

Kwesi offers: "My uncle's gay
but you couldn't tell if you met him.
He's just, like, a regular guy."

This shatters my illusion that
Kwesi is into me.
Kwesi is clearly
a well-meaning straight boy.

"I can only speak for myself,"
Matt says, in a bizarre voice,
like an undercover policeman
pretending to be a gang member.
"I'm not gay, that's all I'm saying."

Matt pats me on the back.
What does this mean?
Go ahead and tell them?

Is this my opportunity
to come out to The Boys?
Was that Matt's blessing?

I scan six pairs of eyes.
It's a moment in time but it's like a lifetime:
Matt, Nathan, Kwesi, Kojo, Abdi, and Sam
wait for me to speak.

I feel a surge of embarrassed heat.
I feel tears welling in my eyes.
I can't cry here in front of The Boys
and everyone in the lunch hall.

Kojo looks away.

Abdi pipes up: "So, Kai, are you gay?"

"Shut up, man," says Sam, nudging Abdi.

Nathan looks from me to Matt,
from Matt back to me,
like a fight is about to break out.

For a moment I think
I might like to fight Matt,
take my chances and throw a punch
at the amateur
boxer.

I feel angry.

I feel pushed under the bus.
I feel pushed out of the closet
because Matt wants to stay inside.
Once I'm out, he'll lock the door
behind me.

I exhale and say, "Yes, I'm gay."

This isn't how I imagined coming out
at school (in the lunch hall on fish and chips Friday),
but I guess this is as good a day as any.

"I knew it!" Kwesi raises a fist.

I flinch automatically,
as if he's gonna punch me.

Kwesi's fist hovers in front of me,
and I realize he wants a fist bump.
"Spud me," he says softly.

Does he feel sorry for me?

As our fists meet,
I see a twinkle in Kwesi's eye.
I make sense to him now.
He no longer has to search
for the answer
to the question of me.

Nathan offers me a fist bump.
Abdi and Sam pat me on the back.

It all feels so convivial,
like The Boys have planned
their perfect reactions.

But then I realize
Kojo hasn't looked at me.
Kojo must've missed the memo.

Give him time, says my angel,
he's no threat to you.

I force a smile for Matt,
who smiles back,
but I have no idea
                    what he's thinking.

I've never felt more
                    distant from him.

While The Boys list
everyone else in our school
known to be LGBTQ+,
I finish my fish and chips in silence.

RAINBOW SPRINKLES–AFTER SCHOOL–
VASS'S BEDROOM

On Vass's bed there are pillows
and colorful cushions galore.

There are posters on the wall,
clothes on the floor,
and a big blue evil eye hanging
above their bedroom door.

"Whipped cream, marshmallows,
and rainbow sprinkles.
The way you both like it."
Theía Estélla hands us
our two hot chocolates.

She's extra tanned from our holiday in Cyprus.
Her classic French manicured nails are perfect.

"Thanks, Mum," mumbles Vass.

"Ευχαριστώ, Θεία Εστέλλα," I thank her.

"Είναι τέλεια," I tell her,
to make up for Vass's distinct lack
of enthusiasm:
Vass isn't usually this dismissive
of their mum.

"Μπράβο, αγόρι μου." Theía Estélla
smiles and pinches my cheek,
the way she often does when I speak Greek.

She leaves the bedroom and shuts the door.

"She doesn't realize we've grown up."
Vass rolls their eyes.

Their whole vibe feels
                    off to me.
I don't know,
maybe Vass and Theía Estélla
have had a row recently?

I look down at the sprinkles
on my marshmallows and whipped cream,
then around Vass's bedroom,
which looks like the wind blew in
Pride parades from decades ago:
a "Pits and Perverts" T-shirt
from Lesbians and Gays Support the Miners,
a SILENCE = DEATH poster,
and five updates of the Pride flag.

"Well, you still love rainbows," I tease,

in an effort to lighten the mood.

"Anyway, where were we?
Oh yeah! You were telling me
how you don't think Kwesi is into you."

"Exactly! Like I said,
I think I misinterpreted
how he was looking at me.
I think he was just trying
to figure me out."

"I know how that feels," says Vass.

I wait for Vass to say more but they don't.

I take a slow sip of my hot chocolate
and the marshmallows tickle my nose.

Vass doesn't seem as excited
about my coming out
as I'd imagined they would be.

Vass's bedroom looks fit for a Pride party,
but Vass isn't celebrating me.

Something about Vass seems
darker these days, like clouds
threatening to rain on a Pride parade.

"What's wrong, Vass?"

"You do realize Matt outed you,
and that's not cool?"

"I wanted to come out.
I've wanted to do it
since before summer.
If anything, I feel sorry for Matt."

"But when you imagined coming out,
was it like that?"

"No, but it's not Matt's fault.
Nathan and Kwesi put us on the spot.
I think Jyoti concluded Matt was gay
because she liked him,
and he wasn't into her."

"You make a lot of excuses for Matt.
I'm starting to think
you really are in love with him."

I wanna tell Vass
I have a crush on Matt, but
I don't plan to act on it
while Matt's in the closet.

I don't tell Vass any of this.
I feel myself get hot with anger.

"Why can't you be happy
for me coming out?" I ask.
"Nothing's good enough for you.

You roll your eyes at your mum
when she brings you hot chocolate.
You know, you haven't even
congratulated me for coming out.
You pick everything apart
until it seems like a bad thing."

It sounds like my devil speaking.
I know my final statement
applies to me more than Vass.
I know I should take it back.

We don't look at each other.

Vass sips their hot chocolate,
and I gulp mine, swallowing
a mouthful of rainbow sprinkles.

SATURDAY: THE NEW BOY–BOULDERING

"Hot new boy alert," Matt whispers in my ear
as our bouldering youth squad gathers
in a circle on the crash mats
for our first session back since
before the summer holiday.

Matt and I haven't spoken
about yesterday in the lunch hall,
and I don't think we will.

What's done is done, says my angel.
Let's try to move on.
This new boy may be the fresh air you need.

The new boy looks mixed, Black and Asian,
like that tennis player Naomi Osaka.

"He *is* hot," I whisper back to Matt.
The new boy smiles when he looks my way,
and I worry he's heard me.

The new boy wears a fresh-out-the-box
youth squad T-shirt: I can see the creases
from where it was folded,
waiting to be claimed
and worn for the first time.

When Matt and I introduce ourselves to him,
we find out his name is Obi
and he's done some bouldering before;
in fact, his private school has its own wall.

"Do you have a boxing gym as well?"
Matt asks Obi enthusiastically.
I can't tell if Matt's flirting or just being friendly.

"Yes, but I don't really go in for contact sports,"
says Obi. "We have a pool, which I use a lot.
My issue with our school's bouldering wall is
they hardly ever change the problems."
He looks at me. "I like new challenges," he says.
"I've heard they switch things up pretty often here?"

"Yes, they do," I answer, feeling aflutter.
"Every few weeks they close one section,
strip it down, and put up new problems."

"That's what I heard," says Obi. "Sounds perfect."

"So, how did you hear about this place?"
Matt interrupts us in a fake-casual voice.

Matt's as keen to figure out Obi as I am.

Never in a million years would I have imagined
Matt and me in competition for the same person.

"Jenny told me about it."
Obi points to Jenny at the top of a wall.

Matt and I privately nicknamed her
Spider Girl before summer
because she's so much better
at bouldering than us,
but also because she always jumps
down from the top of a wall
and lands like a superhero,
rather than climb down
like we're supposed to.

Right on cue, Jenny lands
deftly on the crash mat.
Our youth squad coach has his back to her,
and if he heard her rule-breaking landing,
he's chosen to ignore it.

I'm about to ask Obi how he knows Jenny
when she calls him over.

"Your turn, Obe," says Jenny,
effortlessly cool,
dusting the chalk off her hands.

SUNDAY: TAKE YOUR PICK–MUM'S MARKET STALL

"We need to talk
about your detention," says Mum.

"What about it?
I've served my time already," I say.

Mum shakes her head.
"I should ground you."
She tickles me in my ribs.

I bat her hand away, laughing.
"Stop it, Mum," I say.
"Anyway, you're never home.
Whose house would you ground me at?
Granny's? Yiayia and Bapou's?
Theía Estélla's?"

"Take your pick," says Mum,
digging me in my ribs again.
"Promise you won't

sneak out of school again."

"I promise! I promise!
Please! No more tickling!"

Mum pulls me into a tight squeeze,
then she releases me,
cups my face with her hands,
and covers it with her kisses.

"Promise me," Mum pleads,
"no more getting into trouble."

"Yes, I promise!" I say.

Neither of us cares about potential customers
perusing Mum's handmade jewelry,
candles, and compartments of gemstones.

Sunday on Mum's market stall
is our only regular
mum-and-son quality time.

Two of the customers
standing and gawking
are Jenny and Obi from bouldering.

"Hey, Obi," I say, even though
I've known Jenny far longer.

Obi is holding a loop of jade pendant,
which is one of Mum's bestsellers.

She has dozens in a box under
the white sheet and trestle table,
but she only puts out two at a time.

"Hi, Kai," says Obi. "You know Jenny?"

"Hi, Kai," says Jenny. Unreadable.

I turn to Mum. "This is Jenny and Obi,
I know them both from bouldering.
This is my mum, Irína."

"Shut up!" Jenny gasps at this revelation.
"You're Kai's mum? You look so young!"

"Well, I had him young,"
says Mum truthfully.

"Everything on your stall
is so beautiful," says Obi.

A part of me thinks
he's flirting with Mum.
A part of me thinks
he's flirting with me.

"Thank you, sweetheart," Mum says to him.
"And since you're one of Kai's friends,
you get the friends and family discount."
She gestures to the pendant in his hand.

Obi nods and takes out his phone.

"Great! I'll take it," he says, without asking
how much the discount is.

"Something for you, too, darling?"
my multitasking mum says to Jenny,
while presenting Obi with the card reader.
"Fifty percent off—take your pick."

While Mum and Jenny talk gemstones,
Obi turns to me. "Are you here every week?"

"Yes, every Sunday," I say proudly.

"Great!" says Obi, grinning.
"We'll bring some other friends.
Loads of Jenny's pals
are into gemstones and crystals.
She's just the tip of the iceberg.
We have a coven of witches, tarot readers,
and all sorts in our friend group."

"So, are you and Jenny just friends?" I whisper.

"Best buds since prep school," says Obi.

"Cool," I say, smiling far too widely.

"How about you and . . . ?" Obi hesitates.
"Shit! I'm sorry. I'm blanking on his name.
I want to say Mark?"

"It's Matt. And we're just friends, too."

"Cool," says Obi.
"I guess we're friends now,
since I'm getting
the friends and family discount."

"I guess so," I say. "Unless it turns out
you're one of my dad's other kids
and we're actually half brothers."

Obi tilts his head
to process what I've just said.

I've let out my dark humor too soon.

Mum rarely laughs
at my dark humor.

She says I sometimes take a joke too far across the line.

I worry I've done that this time.
I'm relieved when Obi releases his suppressed laughter.

"My goodness, Kai! You're a hoot!
You're an absolute hoot!"

MONDAY: OUT AND PROUD–LUNCH HALL

"Kai, can I talk to you in private, please?"
says Jyoti sheepishly.

"We've got no secrets here," says Nathan.
He flings an arm over my shoulder
and pulls me closer to him.
"Anything you have to say to our boy Kai,
you can say in front of us all."

I smile at Jyoti with a shrug that says,
Just go with it.

"Um, okay," Jyoti begins.
"I'm a little bit confused."

"Are you gay, too?" Abdi asks Jyoti.

"Abdi, man, let her speak," says Sam.

"No, I'm straight,
which is what you said you were

when I asked you," Jyoti says to me.

I wanna correct Jyoti and remind her
that it was Matt who said that, not me,
but I can't be bothered with pedantry.

"Jyoti, it wasn't your place to speculate
about my sexuality
before I was ready to come out.
But, yes, I'm gay
and I don't care who knows.
I hope that clears up
any confusion you're feeling."

"So, you're gay but Matt isn't?" asks Jyoti.

The Boys and I all turn to Matt
to let him speak for himself.

"Yeah, that's right," says Matt.
"So now you've got your facts straight,
is there anything else
we can help you with today?"

Jyoti's mouth hangs open before
she catches herself and closes it.

She scans our group;
her shoulders drop.
She shakes her head,
turns and walks away.

"Is there anything else
we can help you with today?"
Kwesi parrots Matt
and pats him on the back.

The rest of The Boys
explode with laughter.

I wanna see Matt like the rest of The Boys
who've accepted me for me,
who are ready to defend me,
but I can't help but see Matt differently.
I can't help but feel sad for Matt,
knowing he's still denying his sexuality.

I can't explain it properly,
but whenever Matt denies himself,
it's like he's denying a part of me,
the part of me that wants to love him
as more than friends.

MORE HURT THAN ANGRY–AFTER SCHOOL– GRANNY'S KITCHEN

"Why didn't you tell me the truth?"
T seems more hurt than angry.
"I love you, cuz, and I accept you."

"It wasn't the right time," I say, embarrassed.
Of course T loves and accepts me.

"I hear you, cuz, and I respect that,
but I stopped seeing Jyoti because of it.
And now you've come out at school,
she thinks it makes everything cool."

"Well, I guess it's cool with me," I say.

I knew I was coming out to the entire school
by coming out in the lunch hall
where anyone could've overheard.
"Do you wanna get back with her?" I ask.

"I do." T sighs. "But it's not that simple.

I'm already talking to two other girls."

"Well, can't you just tell them
you're getting back with your girlfriend?"

"Whoa! Whoa! Slow down, cuz.
Jyoti wasn't exactly my girlfriend.
We were just seeing each other,
and when you're seeing someone
you can still talk to other people,
unless you've both agreed not to,
and then you're basically saying
you wanna be boyfriend and girlfriend."
T pauses and grins as he realizes.
"Or boyfriend and boyfriend, in your case."

"Are you giving me dating advice?" I ask.

"Are you dating anyone?" T grins again.

"Not yet, but there's this new boy at bouldering . . ."
I hear Granny's keys in the front door.
T's eyes flash to the door as well.
We silently decide to drop the conversation.

"Help me with my trolley!" hollers Granny.

"Coming, Granny!" T and I say in unison.

The Twins block my path
and jump up for hugs
as Granny lugs her trolley

over the threshold.

"Leave it, Granny," says T,
too commandingly.

"You go in, Granny," I say gently.
"We'll bring the shopping in and unpack it."
I reach down to Olivia and Sophia
and sweep them up into my arms.
"Right after I get some hugs and kisses."

TUESDAY: EYES AND EARS–LUNCH HALL

"Hi, Kai," says Jyoti
as she passes our lunch table.

She wants to be liked, says my angel.

"Hi, Jyoti," I reply, with a pang of guilt
for how rude we were to her yesterday,
but she breezes past us before I can
find the right words for an apology.

You'll get another chance, says my angel.

"Is it true she's seeing your cousin?"
whispers Kwesi as he leans into me.

"How did you know that?" I ask, astonished.

"There are eyes and ears everywhere,"
says Kwesi with an air
of mock-mystery,
his hands opening and closing

in front of his face
like little explosions.

Nathan leans across the lunch table toward us.
"What you man talking about?"

"Kai's cousin and Jyoti," says Kwesi.

"Who's Kai's cousin?" asks Abdi.

Sam whispers to Abdi,
whose eyes widen with surprise.

"That's Kai's cousin?" Abdi says to Sam.

Abdi looks at me quizzically,
but I resist the urge to confront Sam
about what he said about T.

I worry it was something bad.

Eyes and ears everywhere, repeats my devil.

I look at the evil eye bracelet
around my left wrist,
a gift from Mum
that's supposed to protect me.

Whispers and gossip make me feel paranoid
about The Boys,
and the sincerity of their friendship with me.

Matt's been quiet all lunchtime,
and he seems to be fading into the background
as I take center stage in this group.

Matt is sitting beside a quiet Kojo,
who's kept his distance from me
ever since I came out last week.

Kojo hasn't said anything homophobic.
It's not anything the others would notice,
but he makes minimal eye contact with me,
he doesn't speak to me directly,
and he sits as far away from me as possible
without actually leaving our lunch table.

I CAN IF YOU HELP ME–IN THE PARK–
AFTER SCHOOL

"Those monkey bars are too high,"
I tell Olivia
as she climbs the ladder to them.

"I want to try," she replies.

"I don't think you'll be able
to hold on," I warn.

I imagine her losing hold
of the monkey bars.
Falling and landing
with a thud. A flood of tears.

I imagine carrying
her small body,
bruised or bloody,
back to Granny's

or, worse still, having to call

an ambulance,

or take her to the hospital
with a broken limb

or a head injury.

Olivia pauses halfway up,
and looks at me curiously.
Is she disappointed in me?

"I can if you help me," Olivia says.

My heart bursts with purpose:
I'm supposed to be helping
my little cousin to do things,
not discouraging her ambition.

I look around to see
if anyone else heard
what this sassy five-year-old said to me.

T pushes a giggling Sophia on a swing
at the other end of the playground.
"Higher! Higher!" she commands,
her voice carrying on the breeze.

"Okay, I'll help you," I say to Olivia.

I hold her by the waist
and help her to swing
from one monkey bar to the next,

and I keep her suspended in the air
when she loses her grip.

I want her to feel like she can fly.

WEDNESDAY: THE INVITE—LUNCH HALL

"So, is it your party
or your sister's party?" I ask Nathan.

"It's my older sister Nicky's party, but I told her
if my friends can't come the party can't run."

I get a warm feeling from Nathan
referring to me as one of his friends.
Maybe I misjudged this situation.
Maybe The Boys aren't his minions.

"Most of her friends are LGBTQ+," Nathan says,
"so you won't be the only one."

I smile at Matt and Matt smiles back.

My devil wants to tell Nathan
I'm not the only
LGBTQ+ person at this table.

"Sounds fun—I'll come," I say.

Everyone smiles and nods approvingly,
apart from Kojo, who refuses to face me.

Abdi turns to Nathan with a look of concern.
"What do you think would happen
if your mum found out?"

"It's not Nicky's first party.
She has them whenever our mum goes away.
She usually pays me to stay in my bedroom
and not to tell Mum."

"How much?" asks Abdi.

"It started with five pounds when I was twelve,
but I've made her double it each year."

"I'd have taken the forty pounds,"
says Abdi, having done the math super quickly.

My eyes return to Kojo,
like a child's tongue troubling a wobbly tooth.

If Kojo weren't in this group,
wordlessly disapproving of me, I'm sure
I'd feel much more at ease.

If I were a dentist, I'd recommend an extraction,
before the rot sets in.

But Kojo has been one of The Boys for years:
perhaps I'm the one who doesn't belong here.

BEST FRIENDS–AFTER SCHOOL–YIAYIA AND BAPOU'S GARDEN

Vass and I sit in silence on the swings
at the far end of Yiayia and Bapou's garden.

Vass's face is wet from crying,
but their tears have stopped streaming.

I want to tell Vass I feel bad for not realizing
something so serious had happened to them,
but I don't want to make this moment about me.

I don't know what to say.

I don't know whether to ask more questions
or wait for more information.

Eventually, I say, "Thank you for telling me.
And, for what it's worth,
you made the right choice
telling your mum first:
it sounds like she's been amazing.
I wouldn't have known what to do

if you'd told me first."

I feel guilty admitting this,
but it's a truth Vass knows about me:
I don't deal well with stress.
I don't think straight under pressure.
My two main adult role models,
Mum and Granny, don't either.

Vass pulls a small packet of tissues
from their pocket, and there's only one left.
I think of all the tears they must've cried
alone
and with Theía Estélla.
They dab their face dry.
"I thought my mum would blame me."

"It's not your fault, Vass," I say gently.

"I know, but it's not like I'm a virgin."

"That's beside the point," I say too angrily.
I catch myself: I'm angry with the wrong person.
"He had no right to do that to you, Vass.
No one has the right to make you do anything,
regardless of what you've done before."

"I know," says Vass.

They hang their head and begin to cry again.

My whole body shudders involuntarily

the moment Vass isn't looking at me.
It's like I've been holding that shudder in.

I don't want Vass to see
that I feel sick to my stomach,
that I fantasized about having sex with Adonis
at night when I zoomed in on that photo of him.

I feel guilty, disgusted, and confused.

As their best friend,
I wish there was more I could do to support them,
besides listen and reassure them
that it wasn't their fault.

They've already told me
that after discussing it with their mum
they've found a sexual assault support group,
which they plan to go to,
and they're on a waiting list for a therapist.

Vass tells me it felt like they left their body
while it was happening.
"It's called dissociation," they say.

They've decided not to report Adonis
to the police in Cyprus.
I worry about this.
I worry Adonis might
sexually assault someone else,
but I don't feel it's my place to say.
It's Vass's choice, at the end of the day.

I do my best not to think about Adonis.
Vass is my concern, not him.

I rest my hand on Vass's back
between their jutting shoulder blades.
For a few agonizing moments,
we stay like this,
side by side on our swings.

When Vass stands,
I stand with them.
They turn and throw
their arms around me,
and cry even harder
into my shoulder.

I've never been
someone's shoulder
to cry on before.
I recall how Granny
was my shoulder
to cry on recently.

Vass sobs and squeezes me tight.
I squeeze them back.
I rub their back.
"Έλα. Είναι εντάξει, αγάπη μου.
Είναι εντάξει."

Yiayia looks out
from the kitchen window,

but I don't let go.

Yiayia and Bapou don't say much,
even though we all speak the same languages.

If Yiayia and Bapou have opinions about us,
they don't express them in Greek or English.

THURSDAY: OPEN FORUM–LUNCHTIME–
MR. NDOUR'S CLASSROOM

"This is an open forum," says Ms. Sarpong,
her hands wide like she wants to hug us all.
"How does race affect you
inside and outside school?"

"I don't know, miss," says Abdi skeptically.
"This feels like another detention to me."

"Yeah, man!" "Exactly!" say Sam and Kwesi.

Mr. Ndour's nostrils flare
as he struggles to contain his anger.
"The note I put on the system
for your form tutors
said this was voluntary.
If you don't want to be here, Abdi,
you're free to leave.
That goes for all of you."

"Relax, sir," says Nathan boldly.

The rest of The Boys snicker,
while Matt and I groan.

"All right, Nathan. Watch your tone."
Ms. Sarpong takes back control.
"Mr. Ndour is right to make it clear
that you don't have to be here.
Mr. Ndour and I have both given up
our lunchtime to facilitate this space
for you to share your concerns.
I thought I was clear last week
that this would be entirely voluntary,
but I can only apologize
if there's been a miscommunication
or misunderstanding."

"You were clear, miss." I speak up
in Ms. Sarpong's defense.

"Thank you, Kai," she says.
"That's reassuring to hear."

It hadn't even occurred to me before this
that adults might need reassurance from us.

Ms. Sarpong is clearly trying her best,
but I don't know if The Boys or Mr. Ndour
are ready to have this conversation.

FRIDAY: NICKY ANDERSON'S HOUSE PARTY

"Let's go to my bedroom," says Nathan.

"Let's do it," says Kwesi.
"I'm first on the Oculus."

Nathan and Kwesi spring up
from the massive sofa
we're all sitting on. All apart from Kojo,
who's on a footstool.

Matt gives me a gesture,
a flat hand, palm facing down.

The rest of The Boys rise
and follow Nathan and Kwesi.

"Didn't I say he should've taken the money?"
Abdi jokes. "This party's dead."

Sam looks back at me and Matt
on the sofa. "You man coming up?"

"Yeah, just a second," says Matt.

"Are you good, Kai?" Sam's eyes search me.

"Yes, I'm good," I reply.

I'm not sure why
Sam's worried about me:
he hasn't paid much attention to me
before now.

"Good." Sam nods and leaves.

Across the living room,
Nicky Anderson sits on
the lap of her girlfriend,
on an oxblood-red leather armchair,
their group of friends at their feet
on a scattering of floor cushions.

They hold court like a royal couple.
They regale their audience
with a shared story:
Nicky says something,
her girlfriend chips in,
and so, the story goes
back and forth between them.

"I want that one day,"
Matt whispers to me.

This must be the reason
Matt gestured for me
to stay here with him.

"Me too," I say, and I know
we both see the same thing.

SATURDAY: THE PENDANT-BOULDERING

Something from my mum
hangs around Obi's neck.

He wears the loop of jade pendant
from Mum's market stall,
even though we're not supposed to
wear jewelry at bouldering.

Coach doesn't seem to notice.

I notice how often,
even though I stay with Matt
and Obi stays with Jenny,
Obi looks over and smiles at me.
I notice his long canines,
and the wolfish look of him.

His whole vibe has changed
in the space of a week.

He's torn the sleeves off

his youth squad T-shirt
to turn it into a tank top.
I notice his biceps and triceps.
I notice the hair in his armpits.

Most of all, I notice the pendant.

I dream of being as close to Obi
as that lucky pendant gets to be.

SUNDAY: BACK FOR MORE–MUM'S MARKET STALL

"Here, look who's back for more."
Mum nudges me gently with her elbow.
I've not officially come out to her,
but I figure she just knows.

"Back in five," says Mum.
She hands over the card reader and money belt,
and, just like that, she's gone.

"Where are your friends?"
I ask Obi as he reaches me.

"Ouch!" Obi laughs.
"I thought you and I were friends?"

"You promised me witches," I remind him.
"I was hoping to join your coven."

"I was hoping to get you alone,
and it looks like I'm in luck, for now."
He grins, and I swoon at the sight
of those canines up close.

"Why do you want me alone?" I ask.

"Why do you think?" he replies.

I know what Obi may be implying,
but this isn't good enough for me.

I was wrong about Kwesi:
my one-to-watch was
a red herring, a distraction.

I hope Obi will be the real thing.

I want Obi
                 to say it.
I need Obi
                 to say it.

I shrug and feign ignorance.
"*No lo sé*," I say in Spanish.

"*¿Hablas español?*" asks Obi.

"*Sí, un poco*," I reply. "*Es uno . . .*"
I go blank in Spanish.
I go back to English.
"It's one of my GCSEs."

"I do French," Obi says,
with a hint of innuendo,
"but I've been on holiday to Spain
with my family."

"*Con mi familia*," I offer in Spanish.

"*Avec ma famille*," Obi says in French.

I look over his shoulder
to check if Mum or anyone else
is coming this way.

Obi looks at the ground,
and bites his bottom lip.

"But you didn't come here
for language lessons,
or to buy another pendant,
did you?" I ask.

"No, I didn't," he says.
He puts a hand to his chest
where the loop of jade rests.
"I came with Jenny last week
because she told me
you work here on Sundays,
and I was planning
to ask you something,
but I couldn't do it
in front of your mum.

Jenny didn't tell me
you work with your mum.
She said she didn't realize
that was your mum
because your mum
looks so young."

I'm impatient.
"Okay, I get it,
I have a young mum.
Can you hurry up
and ask your question
because my young mum
will be back soon?"

"Erm, sorry," he says.
He clicks his tongue,
like he's forgotten how words work.

"Obi, I don't know Morse code."
My eyes implore him to ask.

So I can say yes.

At the same time, I'm embarrassed
he didn't move to me
with more confidence.

"I'm sorry," Obi apologizes again.
"Shit! I'm sorry.
I'm tongue-tied all of a sudden."

I can't bear the tension,
the embarrassment,
the thought of Mum returning
before Obi manages
to untie his   tongue.

As my eyes urge him on,
I find the question on
the tip of   mine.

So, I ask him: "Obi,
would you like to
go on a date with me?"

BREAKING NEWS

KAI: I've got something to tell you.

MATT: I'm in love with you, too. 😉

KAI: You clown! 🐼

MATT: Look who's talking! Okay, tell me. What is it?

KAI: I'm going on a date with Obi.

MATT: WHAT? REALLY? WHEN?

KAI: Next weekend after bouldering.

MATT: TELL ME EVERYTHING!!!

KAI: He came to Mum's market stall today to ask me, but
he couldn't get the words out.
So, I ended up asking him out.

MATT: I'M SO PROUD OF YOU!!!

KAI: Really?

MATT: Of course. The way he's been looking at you the
past two weeks at bouldering, it was obvious he liked
you.

KAI: I was kinda worried.

MATT: Why?

KAI: I thought you liked him, too.

MATT: I've got eyes, haven't I? 👀 He's obviously hot but
even if I did like him, it was clear he liked you and not
me.

KAI: So, you're okay with it?

MATT: Of course! So, where's the posh boy taking you?

KAI: I'm taking him to a place I've been to before with my mum.
He's vegan.
So, I thought I'd start with a vegan place for our first date.
Before I reveal that I'm actually a massive carnivore. 🍗 🥩

MATT: Do you think that'll be a deal-breaker?

KAI: I hope not.

matt: THIS IS SO EXCITING! YOU ONLY JUST CAME OUT LAST WEEK AND NOW YOU'RE GOING ON YOUR FIRST DATE!

kai: I KNOW!!!
WHAT IS LIFE 🐾

THE FOLLOWING SATURDAY:
A SAUCY FIRST DATE

"Don't worry! It's all vegan,"
I reassure Obi as he studies the menu
with a frown of concentration.
"When my mum first brought me here
and I saw names like chick'n and f'sh,
I thought it was real chicken and fish."

"I know it's vegan," says Obi.
"I was looking for something
that isn't a meat substitute.
I didn't become vegan to eat fake meat."

"We can go somewhere else if you'd like?"

"No, I'm sorry. It's all right," he says.
"I'm not really that hungry anyway.
I'll just get some sweet potato fries."

"You sure? The chick'n burger is decent,
especially with the buffalo sauce,

and the f'sh and chips are my favorite,
especially with the tartar sauce."

"What I'm hearing is you rate the sauces
more than the food." Obi laughs.

His laughter reassures me
he's happy to be here with me.

"I guess I have a thing for sauces,"
I say, in a bizarre attempt to flirt.

"Oh yeah?" Obi takes the bait.
"What's your favorite one?"

"My top three in no particular order are:
sweet chili, peri-peri, and mango chutney."

Obi starts to laugh, then covers his mouth,
and I wonder if he's conscious of his toothy smile.

"Did you just call mango chutney
a sauce?" Obi laughs again, and snorts this time.

I feel heat rise in my body
as I realize Obi is laughing at me, not with me.
"Yes," I say uncertainly.

"But it's literally called chutney," says Obi.
"A sauce is something like ketchup or mayo."
He points to them, between us on the restaurant table.
"Or sweet chili and peri-peri, like you said.

But a chutney is a chutney, like a salsa is a salsa,
and neither of those are sauces."

I let out a long sigh.
This level of pedantry could kill any vibe.
Plus, I don't think
what he's saying is correct.

"Shit! I'm sorry," says Obi.
"I'm being a dick, aren't I?"

I make a pinching gesture
with my thumb and index finger
in front of my face.
"A little bit," I say.

"I'm sorry," Obi says again.
"Jenny tells me I can be
a bit of a dick sometimes.
I'm really sorry, Kai.
How about we just order now?"

"Okay," I say nonchalantly.

"Sorry to bother you," Obi begins
as he calls over the waiter.

The way Obi says sorry so often
kinda gives me the ick,
but I try my best to ignore it.

Matt tells me I get irritable

and angry when I'm hungry.

After the waiter takes our order,
Obi leans forward and says,
"So, tell me about you, Kai."

His eyes search my face as he waits
with his elbows on the table between us
and his chin resting in the hammock
made by his long, interlaced fingers.

Obi looks more relaxed now,
which oddly puts me on edge.
"I don't know where to start."

"Family? Heritage?
Favorite subjects at school?
Any hobbies other than bouldering?
Tell me anything."

I relax into telling Obi
about Yiayia, Bapou, and Granny,
Cyprus and Jamaica,
English and drama,
reading, writing, and watching films.

Our food arrives,
and Obi tells me about his parents,
his big brother, who is also queer,
his grandparents in China and Nigeria,
music and French,
and his folk punk band, FRSH MNT T.

"We're called Fresh Mint Tea," says Obi,
"but it's written all in capital letters
without the vowels."

My turn to stifle a laugh.

"And pray tell,
what would your band be called?"
Obi asks me.

"Saucy Saucy Mango Chutney," I reply,
proud of my callback.

"Nice one." Obi smiles
and flashes those sexy canines again.

"I'm glad I asked you on this date," I say,
"and didn't wait for you to ask me."

Obi laughs. "I'm glad, too.
You're funny and forthright."
He pauses. "And very cute."
He pops a sweet potato fry into his mouth.

"Oh, to be a sweet potato fry," I flirt again.

"Oh my! Kai, did you really say that?"
he mock-gasps, and grasps the pendant
like he's clutching a string of pearls.

"I guess I did." I laugh, proud of myself.

"Wow, you're so bold."
He rubs the pendant
between his thumb and index finger.

"Do you like it?" I ask.

"This pendant," he replies,
"or your flirting?"

I shake my head and roll my eyes:
he knows what I mean.

"Yeah, I like it," he says,
with his dog-toothed smile.

His foot finds mine under the table.
"I like you, Kai.
Me gustas mucho."

Oh,   Obi.

I feel a different kind
of heat rise in my body,
from my feet to my blushing face.
"*¡Muy bien!*" I say.
"I like you a lot, too."

I feel so lucky.
I feel surer about Obi
than I ever did about Matt or Kwesi.
I could never have imagined this moment
happening with either of them.

I can barely believe it's happening
with Obi right now.

MONDAY: DOE-EYED–AFTER SCHOOL– VASS'S BEDROOM

Sometimes, I think I see flashes
of the assault in Vass's big brown eyes,
like a deer in headlights,
but I could be imagining it.

Vass doesn't talk about it directly,
not since they told me on the swings,
but we talk about things related to it.

We talk about the support group
they go to once a week,
but I only get the gist of it,
without any details
of these people to hold on to.

They're important to Vass,
but Vass can't share them with me.
It's like a portal to another world,
or a layer of reality I can't see.

"When do I get to meet
this anxious young man?"
Vass asks me when I tell them
about my date with Obi,
and read them a poem
I wrote about him.

"I don't know," I say.
"It was just one date."

"I can't wait to check out those fangs
you're so obsessed with."

"I'm not obsessed," I protest,
"and I didn't call them fangs."

Vass snatches my notebook
and finds the page I just shared.

"Right there:
'his dog-toothed smile,' you said."
Vass quotes me back to myself.
"Woof, woof." Vass teases me.

When I've recovered from
the biggest cringe of my life,
Vass looks at me, doe-eyed.

"I'm so happy for you, Kai."

Vass may not be able to share
everything with me,

but I'm happy I can still share
everything with them.

"If you really wanna meet Obi,"
I say, as the idea comes to me,
"you could come to bouldering."

Vass tilts their head
as they consider my invitation
with an unreadable expression.

"Matt's been wanting to meet you, too,"
I add, as if this would sweeten the deal.

But this isn't about Matt or Obi.
It's about Vass and me.

I wanna spend as much time
with Vass as possible,
especially when
they seem so vulnerable.

SATURDAY: I CAN'T EVEN THINK STRAIGHT– BOULDERING

Vass wears rainbow leggings
and a tank top that says:
"I Can't Even Think Straight."

Their long hair is in a high ponytail.

Jenny and Obi compliment Vass
on their outfit and rainbow-colored nails.

It's the first time in ages
I've seen Vass with short nails.

Coach hands Vass a fresh-out-the-box
youth squad T-shirt to change into.

Vass holds the T-shirt at arm's length
between their thumb and index finger,
like it's the tail of a small, dead rodent.

"This is a hate crime," jokes Vass.

Jenny, Obi, and several others laugh.

Matt shakes his head disapprovingly
and looks at me sternly,
as if Vass's sense of humor is my fault.

Visibly flustered,
our usually unbothered coach
explains that the purpose
of the youth squad T-shirts
is to tell the teens
apart from the adults.
"It's part of our child-protection policy,"
Coach says earnestly.

"I was only joking," says Vass.
They pull the youth squad T-shirt on
over their tank top.

"Nothing to say you can't customize it,"
Obi says to Vass, as a consolation.
His thumbs point back to himself
sporting his own sleeveless version.

"Give us a twirl," I tell Obi, as a joke.

To my surprise, Obi twirls,
like a well-trained puppy.

Woof, woof, Vass mouths at me.

We come together in a group of five.

Jenny drawn to Vass. Obi drawn to me.
Matt's not saying much to anyone.

I thought Matt was dying to meet Vass,
but Jenny and Obi are much friendlier.

My devil tells me to ignore Matt.

My angel tells me to focus on Vass.

The advice is almost the same,
but the second feels more kind.

We take each problem in turn.
Jenny, the most experienced, goes first.
Next is Obi, then Matt, then me.
Vass goes last each time,
to see how we handle each problem.

They get the hang of it in no time.
Their long arms have a wide reach,
and their rainbow legs stretch,
like a ballet dancer suspended in midair.

"You're doing so well for a beginner,"
says Jenny to Vass encouragingly.

"Thanks, babe," says Vass from on high,
at the top of the wall.

Vass doesn't jump to the crash mat, like Jenny,
but climbs down cautiously,

and is met with a high five from Obi.

When I offer them a high five,
Vass throws their arms around me.
"This is so much fun," they say.
"Thank you for inviting me!"

CHECKING IN

KAI: Are you okay?

MATT: Yeah.

KAI: You sure?

MATT: Yeah.

KAI: Come on. Be honest.

MATT: Why don't you just say what you wanna say.

KAI: Fine. You weren't very friendly to Vass today.

MATT: I knew you were gonna say that.

KAI: So, what's your problem with them?

MATT: I don't have a problem with them. But I've never met anyone like Vass before. I didn't know what to say.

KAI: You could've at least said "well done" a few times.
I've told you lots about them.
You knew what to expect.

MATT: It's one thing to hear about them and to see
people like them online, but when they turned up
wearing that tank top and rainbow leggings, it was a bit
much for me.

KAI: Look at how friendly Spider Girl and Obi were.

MATT: Of course you'd think your posh new boyfriend
behaved perfectly.

KAI: I said SG *and* Obi. I'm not comparing you to Obi.
I just hoped you'd be nicer to Vass.

MATT: I'm sorry. I didn't mean to upset you or Vass.
Did Vass say something?

KAI: No, they didn't say anything, but I didn't bring it up.
I didn't wanna draw any attention to how weird you
were being.

MATT: So, Vass didn't say they thought I was rude?

KAI: No, they didn't say anything about you.
They said they had fun.

MATT: Okay. Good. I'm sorry I was weird.
I'm glad Vass had fun. I'll make more of an effort with
them next time.

KAI: You'd better.

MATT: I will. I promise.

KAI: Okay. Good.

MATT: It's just hard for me to see someone so comfortable with themselves.

KAI: I know. But it's still no excuse to be rude.

MATT: I know. I really am sorry.

KAI: By the way, Obi isn't my boyfriend. We're just seeing each other.

MATT: But do you want him to be your boyfriend?

KAI: Yes, I do. I really do.

SUNDAY: FEAR OF MISSING OUT–MUM'S MARKET STALL

I'm confused as I see Vass, Jenny, and Obi
walking toward me.

"Έλα, Βασιλιώ μου!" says Mum,
before I have a chance to speak.
"Έλα," Mum says again,
darting to the front of the trestle table.
"Μάνα μου! It's so good to see you!"
She squeezes Vass.

"Καλησπέρα, Θεία Ιρίνα," says Vass, breathless.
"It's good to see you, too."

Jenny and Obi watch,
as if this is the cutest thing they've ever seen.

Mum releases Vass and acknowledges them:
"Jenny and Obi, isn't it?"

"Well remembered, Irína," says Obi.

I laugh and ask Obi: "Have you three
been hanging out without me?"

"We met up at the station," says Obi,
"and came straight here to see you."

"You know I'm working today," I say
as I make my way round to the front of the table.

"I can spare you for an hour or two," says Mum.
"As long as you come back to help me pack up."

I wanna spend as much time
with Vass as possible
and today there's the added
incentive of Obi,
but Sunday on Mum's market stall is as sacred to me
as going to church is sacred to Matt.

I feel FOMO creeping in
at the thought of saying no to them
and staying with Mum.

I feel annoyed with all three of them
for putting me in this position,
to have to choose between them and Mum.

"We'll all help to pack up," says Obi,
grinning at me, pleased with himself,
like he's single-handedly solved world peace.

I'm amused and no longer annoyed.
Obi's innocent charm disarms me,
like he's some sort of Disney prince.

Vass and Jenny nod in agreement.

"That's sorted, then."
Mum shoos us away.
"Have a nice time."

"Righto. Cheerio," Obi says to Mum.

Her eyes widen in disbelief.

"Cheerio," Mum repeats. "Actually, hold on, kids!"

She pulls two tens from her money belt.
She hands one to me and another to Vass.
Then two more: one to Jenny and another to Obi.

"Okay, then." Mum smiles at me mischievously.
"Off you go."

I'm slow to do the math.
As I walk away with Vass, Jenny, and Obi,
I realize the four of us are sharing the forty pounds
Mum usually gives me for my work every Sunday.

I laugh to myself.
I turn and wave at Mum,
who waves back
and sticks out her tongue.

Maybe Mum will give me
another thirty pounds later,
but even if she doesn't,
three-quarters of my pocket money
is a small price to pay
for more time with Vass,
for more time with Obi.

MONDAY: THE AUTHOR TALK–
ASSEMBLY HALL

The Boys look my way
when the visiting author in assembly
casually says he's gay.

"Settle down, boys," says Mr. Ndour.
This draws The Author's attention,
when he probably wouldn't have noticed.

The Author pauses.
I feel embarrassed for him, and for me.

The Boys and Mr. Ndour have interrupted
The Author's time in the spotlight.

The Author told us at the start of his talk
that he still gets nervous.
His nostrils flare as he pushes out air.
He's pissed off.
I worry he might think one of us
said something homophobic about him,

thanks to Mr. Ndour's overreaction.

"As I was saying," The Author continues,
"when I was at school,
there was a law called Section 28,
which prohibited the promotion of homosexuality
which, among other things, meant
you wouldn't see LGBTQ+ books in school,
you wouldn't have a visiting author like me,
and teachers couldn't tell students
it's okay to be gay.
This law was in place from 1988,
when I was four,
until it was repealed in 2003,
when I was eighteen.
That was my entire school career."

The phrase "school career"
sounds kinda odd to me.

It sounds like being at school counts as a job,
which I guess is kinda true,
because it can be hard work
when students gossip about you
or teachers have it in for you.

I want The Author's job.
But I don't raise my hand
when the time comes
to ask him questions about it.
I'm still too embarrassed
by the negative attention.

I look down and twist
the evil eye bracelet
around my left wrist.

Luckily, The Author's responses
to other people's questions go a long way
to telling me what I need to know:

"When you have a book written,
you send the first three chapters to an agent
with a synopsis of the entire plot,
along with a cover letter about yourself.

"Read widely in different genres.
Fiction and nonfiction, prose and poetry,
scripts, food writing, travel writing:
anything you can get your hands on."

"Some of my favorite writers are
Benjamin Zephaniah, James Baldwin,
and Michael Rosen."

"Talk to Mrs. James, your school librarian,
about what you've read and enjoyed,
and what your writing ambitions are.
She'll have lots of recommendations."

Here, The Author points to Mrs. James,
off to the side, who beams with pride.
Both her massive smile and her Progress
Pride flag badge on her staff lanyard.

"The majority of writers don't do it full-time.
Those who do are often supported
by family money or the income of their partner.
I'm fortunate to be a full-time writer now,
but I lived at home with my mum until recently.
Before I published my second book,
I had several other jobs alongside writing,
such as retail, waiting tables, and bar work.

"I usually write one book at a time
but some writers I know
will have two, three, four or more
books on the go at once."

"For me, it's a few years between
when I start writing a new book
and it being available in shops."

"My agent gets me a book deal,
which means a publisher
agrees to publish my book,
then I work with an editor,
and sometimes an assistant editor,
to make the book better."

"Sometimes a lawyer or sensitivity reader
checks the book to make sure
it won't get me into any trouble."

"There's usually a copy editor and proofreader
to catch any spelling and grammar mistakes,
and to make sure the text looks correct in print."

"Some of my books have illustrations,
and it's important to me
that illustrators are credited properly.

"There's design, production, publicity,
marketing, and many more jobs in publishing
besides being an author."

"In mainstream publishing there's a massive team
involved in getting books ready for release,
as well as promoting them to readers."

It sounds so much bigger than I imagined,
with so many different people
working alongside The Author,
each with their own role to play.

I feel embarrassed
not to have known this.
I feel angry without knowing why.

Then I remember last year
Mum wouldn't take a day off
to take me to an exhibition
about Malorie Blackman
and the power of stories
at the British Library.
Even though Mum knows
I wanna be an author
and Malorie is one of my favorites.

I made sure to tell Mum
the exhibition was free entry
in case she was worried
it would cost lots of money.
But all she was worried about
was the loss of earnings
if she didn't do her stall.

She told me I could go
on my own or with a friend.
But I didn't want to go
on my own or with a friend.
I wanted to go with her.

I wanted Mum to show me
she's as "invested" in me
as she claims to be.
I wanted Mum to show an interest
in what's important to me.

I could've asked Matt or Vass to go with me,
but I chose to stay angry at Mum.

I didn't go at all.
As the saying goes:
I cut off my nose
to spite my face.

"That'll be you one day,"
Matt whispers encouragingly.

Mr. Ndour coughs. His eyes shoot daggers at us.

The bell goes with hands still raised.

"That's all we have time for, I'm afraid,"
Mr. Ndour says, gesturing for everyone
to put their hands down.

I shuffle down the aisle
toward the double doors of the assembly hall.

I overhear Mr. Ndour say this to The Author:
"I'm sorry about the poor behavior
of some of our boys.
I'll be having words with them and their parents.
That group has been acting up lately."

I wanna dash my backpack at Mr. Ndour's head,
but it's heavy with books and could do real damage.
I'd get worse than a detention,
I'd probably be suspended or expelled.
The police could be called in.
I could be charged with assault.

I grip the strap of my heavy backpack and walk on.
I don't know why I get so angry so often.

Out in the corridor I still feel hot with rage.
What's Mr. Ndour's problem?
Apart from leaving school that one time at lunchtime,
what have we done to deserve being bad-mouthed?

I feel more embarrassed than before.

Mr. Ndour is out of order.

The Boys are waiting for me
halfway down the corridor.

"Mr. Ndour's a dickhead," I say loudly.
The Boys burst into surprised laughter,
and I feel a bit better.

Nathan pats my back.
Kwesi drapes an arm over my shoulder.
He keeps it there as we stalk the corridor
together, looking out for our next laugh.

Abdi says another mean thing about Mr. Ndour
and it's like a bomb has gone off:
we're a mess of flailing limbs,
our laughter bouncing off the walls.

"All of you, hurry up and get to class!"
shouts Mrs. James behind us.

MEET THE AUTHOR–LUNCHTIME–THE LIBRARY

The Author is selling and signing books
in the library at lunchtime,
but I feel too embarrassed to wait in line
in case he remembers me as one of the boys
Mr. Ndour pointed out as acting up.

The Author's book is on display
with the other LGBTQ+ books.
Something about this makes me feel
uncomfortable on his behalf.

I spot Jyoti in line, so I ask her,
"Will you get one signed for me?"
I hold out a ten, one-quarter of
my pocket money, at arm's length.

Jyoti turns to some younger kids behind her
and says, "You don't mind if Kai joins me, do you?"
It's not a question and we all know it.
They shrug and go back to chatting.

"Can you just get it signed?" I ask again.
"I'm too embarrassed from assembly."

"But you've said
you want to be an author,
and you're gay.
And here's a gay author.
You've got to take the opportunity
when it's in front of you."

I take plenty of opportunities, I think.
I took the opportunity to come out to The Boys.
I took the opportunity to ask out Obi.

"What's the opportunity here?" I ask Jyoti.

"You can ask him to read your work,"
Jyoti says, like it's obvious.
"You can ask him to mentor you
or introduce you to his agent."

The line shuffles forward
and so does Jyoti.
She feels a million steps ahead of me.

"I'm not ready for any of that," I say.
"I just want a signed book.
I haven't even read this book.
It might not be any good."

I laugh and so does Jyoti.

It makes me happy to make her laugh.

She's a sweet person,
if a little try-hard sometimes,
and a massive gossip.

She remembered that I wanna be an author,
but I've no idea what she wants to be. So, I ask her.

"Do you wanna be an author, too?"

"I've always thought I wanted to be
a journalist because I love stories.
Stories about people in particular,
and I like to know what's going on."

I can't resist teasing her a bit.
"You mean you like to gossip?"

"You could call it that." Jyoti smirks.

"I call it gossip," I tell her,
"because that's what it is."

For a moment I worry I'm being too harsh,
but Jyoti laughs again.

"Anyway," she continues,
"I was about to say I found it interesting
when The Author talked about
his relationship with his editor.
I like the idea of helping

someone to tell their story,
to make it clear and compelling.
It was fascinating to me
when he said sometimes reality
is less convincing than fiction."

"Yes, I bet it was," I say,
with a bombastic side-eye
as I kiss my teeth at her.

We both laugh.

The line shuffles forward again;
we shuffle forward, too.

Jyoti gives me a wry smile.
"You know, if you're looking
for an editor for your writing,
I'd be happy to take a look."

I'm warmed by Jyoti's offer,
but I'm not ready to take her up on it.
I'm not sure I trust her yet:
I could happily hand her a ten-pound bill,
but I couldn't imagine
handing her my notebook.
I guess my face shows it.

"No pressure," Jyoti says, smiling
but crestfallen.
"I just thought I'd put it out there.
I'm going to ask The Author

if he can arrange for me
to do work experience with his editor."

We shuffle forward for a third time,
and now there are only two students
between us and The Author.

Mrs. James takes my ten,
and gives me my change:
one pound and one penny.
She writes my name on a sticky note,
to make sure The Author spells it correctly.

Then the same again for Jyoti.

I decide to stay in line with her
to meet The Author.

ANOTHER DETENTION–AFTER SCHOOL

"This isn't fair," I tell Mr. Ndour,
and The Boys all agree with me,
apart from Kojo, who sits silently.

Mrs. James reported us all to Mr. Ndour
because she didn't see
which one of us said he was a dickhead.

"Settle down, boys," says Mr. Ndour.
Like a broken record or a boring song,
Mr. Ndour repeats
the same dry lyrics
day in and day out.

"For fuck's sake, man," I say.
"Okay, it was me," I blurt out.

The classroom falls silent,
and it's like time stands still.

I know my confession

is wholly unnecessary.

Nathan already told me
The Boys would take the fall with me.

I don't quite understand
what's brought on their loyalty to me.

Was it the police stop
and our first detention together?

My coming out as gay
and going to Nicky Anderson's house party?

Or is it just because
I make them laugh?

Real time resumes.

"Ms. Sarpong's office." Mr. Ndour points
to his classroom door.
His nostrils flare a warning.

"Gladly," I say, and I stand.
My plastic-and-metal school chair
tips and falls backward,
and I can't be bothered to pick it up.

I pick up my backpack,
which is even heavier now
with one more book,
signed by The Author.

I know better than to throw my backpack.
I know I have a bright future,
no matter what
this one teacher thinks of me.

I step into the empty corridor.

The Boys begin to mutter.

"Silence right now!" Mr. Ndour yells,
and The Boys obey.

TUESDAY: THE GOOD ONE–AFTER SCHOOL AT GRANNY'S

T's taken The Twins to the park.

"You're supposed to be the good one, Malachi.
Now me have to worry about you, too?"
asks Granny, standing over me.

I don't answer her.
I sit silent and still
at the empty kitchen table.

Dinner's cooked, but it won't be served
until my cousins return.

My belly's growling
and my head is aching.

Granny's been yelling for half an hour already,
about how I swore at Mr. Ndour,
and threw a chair across his classroom.
Neither of which is true.

I didn't swear directly at him.
I didn't throw my chair: it fell over.
But Granny's not giving me
the benefit of the doubt.
Granny's never been angry at me, not like this.
It feels shitty and now I understand
why T has always been so envious of me.

I think of Sam whispering
something to Abdi about T.
His reputation has traveled
all the way to my school.

I'm sick of being the good one.
I never asked to be the good one.

Maybe I'm not all that good.
Maybe I just have a cousin
who people think of as bad.

I should be allowed to make mistakes, too.

I never claimed to be good,
but I've benefited from being
seen as better behaved than T.

Granny shouts at T like this all the time,
without listening to his side of the story.

Ms. Sarpong phoned Granny
when she couldn't get hold of Mum.

Apparently, Mr. Ndour's fiction
is more convincing than reality.
Mr. Ndour, the snake, phoned Ms. Sarpong
when I was walking to her office.
Ms. Sarpong wouldn't listen to me.
Ms. Sarpong had said I could talk
to her "about anything."
But "anything" clearly didn't include
one of her teachers having a vendetta
against me and The Boys.
Ms. Sarpong said I had "an attitude,"
which maybe I do and maybe I did in that moment.
She cut me off with a raised hand.
"Okay, Malachi, that's enough," said Ms. Sarpong.
"You need to calm down now."

Granny shows no signs of calming down,
now or anytime soon.

I know Granny feels under pressure
because the school contacted her.

I know Granny feels afraid
I'll become another troublesome grandson.

I stay silent and still at the kitchen table.
I slump in my seat as Granny continues to shout.

I dissociate.
I leave Granny and my body behind.

I sink underwater,

and I can't hear Granny clearly anymore,
besides the occasional swear word
in explicit and explosive plosive patois,
which hit me like big, bad bullets
piercing the surface of my swimming pool of solitude,
wounding me
even though I'm in denial
and refuse to believe
words can hurt.

I'm surrounded by red and blue,
like blood suspended in water.

I stay there until my cousins return.
All three of them laughing.

T chases The Twins into the kitchen.

Granny's stopped shouting.
She's plating our dinner now.

The giggling twins climb onto my lap,
where I'm still seated at the kitchen table.

The Twins bring me back into my body.

"Kai's home base," Olivia says to T.
"Kai's home base." Sophia clings to me.

T takes out his phone.
I smile for the photo
T takes of me and The Twins.

I begin our special greeting:
"Hello there, my favorite girls
in the whole wide universe."

"It's world, not universe,"
they say, making my day.

T smiles at me kindly
and, for the first time,
I think I see him clearly.

If all our lives

I was supposed to be

the good one,

what was T supposed to be?

IT TAKES A VILLAGE–NIGHTTIME–MY BEDROOM

"I don't care if Granny already shouted at you,
it's my turn now!" Mum yells at me.

"No, that's not how this works!"
I yell back. "You missed your turn!
I only get to see you at night,
when we're both tired and grumpy,
or on Sundays when I have to
earn my keep on your market stall,
working for room and board
like I'm in a Charles Dickens novel.
You work full-time, study part-time,
but you're a mum none of the time.
You're never around for me!
The school couldn't get hold of you,
that's why they had to phone Granny!"

"Excuse me, Malachi Michaelides,
you can dial down your bloody sass.
I'm not having that from you today.

Don't you dare come for me!
You know it takes a village to raise a child,
and you have me and Granny,
Yiayia and Bapou and Theía Estélla, too.
We could've spent time together in Cyprus
but you went off with Vass every day.
So, don't you dare tell me I've missed my turn.
The bloody cheek of you!
Every person I've mentioned
has my permission to tell you off
for your poor behavior,
bad judgment, and bloody attitude.
We'll take turns one by one.
We'll come down on you
all at once like a ton of bricks.
I'll get your dad involved if I have to.
I'll do whatever it takes to protect you.
Every one of us is invested in you.
In your future and your safety."

A tear falls from Mum's right eye,
followed by more from both eyes.

The pressure of parenting me is too much for her.

I wanna cry as well, but I don't.
I wanna wipe Mum's tears away, but I don't.

I feel myself shaking with anger
at Mum's threat to involve my dad.

What has he ever invested in me?

If all the people who care for me
were bricks with which to build
a home, my dad   could only be
the space for a door or a window.

"Can you at least let me tell you
what actually happened?" I plead.
"Because the school's got it twisted!"

"Malachi!" Mum commands
with tear-streaked fury.
"I listened to your version of events
when you strolled out of school
and got stopped by the police.
You promised me
no more getting into trouble.
I feel like such a fool
for not coming down harder on you."

"But, Mum, I promise, this was different.
Please, will you just listen to me?"

Mum sighs a heavy Mum sigh.
She wipes the tears from her eyes.
She runs her fingers
through her long, straight hair
and scratches her skull
as if to settle her thoughts.
She does this twice more,
then shakes off her anger
with a shudder of her shoulders.

Mum doesn't say anything for a few long seconds.
Then she fixes her eyes on me
and says, "Go on, I'm listening."

I know I'm lying
as I hear myself say,
"Mr. Ndour is picking on me
because I'm gay . . ."

EYE FOR AN EYE

MATT: Why did you have to lie to your mum? The truth would've been enough. I could've backed you up as well. You could've called me. I would've spoken to Auntie Irína. I was there and I know you didn't swear directly at Mr. Ndour. And I saw how your chair fell over.

KAI: He lied about me first. He said I swore at him and threw the chair across his classroom. So, he's getting a taste of his own medicine. My mum's taking tomorrow morning off work. And she's coming into school to speak to Ms. Sarpong.

MATT: You went too far to say you think he's targeting you for being gay. I don't think he was being homophobic.

KAI: You don't know for sure, do you? You've not come out, so you don't face the discrimination I do.

MATT: You're weaponizing your sexuality to get your way. What if Mr. Ndour loses his job?

KAI: He's not gonna lose his job.

MATT: How do you know for sure?

KAI: I don't care. He lied about me.

MATT: An eye for an eye will leave the whole world blind.

KAI: Are you seriously quoting the Bible at me?

MATT: No, it's Mahatma Gandhi.

KAI: I'm not launching a campaign for India's
independence from British rule.
I'm just trying to get one teacher off my back at school.

MATT: You just googled Gandhi, didn't you?

KAI: Yes, I did.

MATT: There's still time to tell your mum the truth.

KAI: Which is?

MATT: You didn't swear directly at Mr. Ndour. And your
chair fell over when you stood up to leave the classroom.
You don't know why he lied about it. But you have no
reason to think he was being homophobic.

LATER THAT NIGHT: EAR TO THE DOOR–
MUM'S BEDROOM

I tiptoe toward
Mum's closed bedroom door.
I press my ear to it.
Mum speaks in Greek
but too quiet and quick
for me to catch
most of what she says.
The few words I hear
are swear words.
I hope her swearing
is about Mr. Ndour
and not me.

I knock.

I hear footsteps.
Mum opens the door
with her phone
still at her ear.
"I'll call you back, Estélla."

In the doorway,
I explain my lie
and Mum listens,
her face blank,
as if her emotions
are still loading.

"I don't deserve this," she says.
Her voice and face break.
Nostrils flare, lips twitch, eyes well up.
"I don't deserve to be lied to.
Not by you.
I'm on your side, Malachi.
I was ready to go to war for you."

"I know," I say. "I'm sorry."

I wait but Mum doesn't respond.

"Do you forgive me?" I ask,
fearful and uncertain
of what Mum thinks of me.

She doesn't answer
with words. She flings
her arms around me.
Squeezes me tight.

WEDNESDAY: THE TRUTH WILL SET YOU FREE–
BEFORE SCHOOL

Matt laughs to himself
as he approaches me before school
at the gates of our weekday prison.
"There's the boy who almost cried wolf!"

I shake my head at him.
We walk through the gates and out of earshot
of our prison-guard teachers
and fellow-inmate students.

"Oh no! Not you!" I chuckle.
"I hate Pastor Matthew!" I say this
but I mean the opposite.

Matt does this church pastor comedy character
because he thinks it gives me the ick
but really, I love him.
The character, that is.

"Excuse me,

young man," Pastor Matthew continues.
"I think the words
           you're looking for
are
           'Thank you'
and
           'I love you.'"

Did Matt say that last part in his own voice?

I'm too shocked to say anything.

"So, how did Auntie Irína react?" Matt asks.

I must've imagined that last part.

"She was angry I made up the homophobia part,
but also relieved I owned up,
you know, before it blew up—"

"My thoughts exactly," Matt interrupts me.

"But wait, listen: she said she was glad
she didn't come into school this morning
like a crazy Karen peddling fake news."

Matt creases over with laughter.
I feel proud and warmed to have achieved
a second big laugh from Matt
before the school day has begun.

"Wow!" Matt says, recovering.

"Your mum called herself a Karen.
Auntie Irína's too funny, man!"

I don't mind sharing the credit
for this laughter with Mum.
We're a team, at the end of the day.

I tell Matt how Mum will still
email Ms. Sarpong to complain
about Mr. Ndour, but only
with the facts of the matter
and nothing about homophobia.

"You happy with that?" asks Matt.

"Yes. At least Mum's on my side now."

Matt reaches forward
and puts his hands on my shoulders,
and says, in all sincerity,
"Didn't I say the truth would be enough?
The truth will set you free."
He squeezes my shoulders,
and then releases them.

I give my closeted gay friend a look that says,
I'm not gonna say it.

Matt gives me a look back that says,
Thank you for not saying it.

"You know what I didn't realize

until afterward?" I ask him.

"What?" Matt sounds worried.

"I officially came out to my mum
by telling her I thought Mr. Ndour
had been homophobic to me.
My official coming out to my mum
was overshadowed by a lie."

"That's kinda messed up,"
Matt says sympathetically.

"It's really messed up," I agree.

My devil reminds me
I should still be angry at Matt,
because my coming out at school
has been undermined by the lie
I'm keeping for him.

"Better luck next time."
Matt pats me on the back.
"You've still got plenty
of people left to come out to:
your yiayia and bapou,
your granny, your dad,
and your family in Jamaica."

The rage I feel at the mention of my dad
surpasses any anger I feel for Matt.
I feel my eyes well up and my face flush.

My dad who doesn't help Mum,
and has next to nothing to do with me.
My dad who Mum threatened
to get involved in order to protect me.
I feel like I'm falling into a pit,
into the Earth's core full of magma.

Matt puts his hands back on my shoulders.
"Kai, come back."

My shoulders soften,
                and I can breathe again.

I didn't realize
                I hadn't been breathing.

Matt smiles at me gently.
                He waits for me.

Over his shoulder, a flow
of students enter the school gates.
Matt doesn't seem to mind.

I dare to dream that,
in time,
Matt could be mine.

"I wanna come out to my granny,"
I say, finding the thread
of our conversation again.
"I'm not bothered about my dad,"
I lie, willing it to be true.

"I don't think I'll come out
to my family in Jamaica.
You know it's illegal there."

Matt gives my shoulders
a longer squeeze this time,
before he releases them,
like he didn't wanna let go.

"You know it's not illegal to be
a gay person in Jamaica."
Matt corrects me unnecessarily,
as if I didn't know this.
"It's illegal to have gay sex.
That's illegal in Nigeria as well."

"I know," I say, giving bombastic side-eye,
but relieved to be back
in this conversation with Matt
and not lost in my anger.
"But I do plan to have gay sex, someday."

"Someday soon?" asks Matt.
"With Obi, maybe?"

"Maybe," I reply, looking Matt in the eye.

The truth will set you free, Matt said,
but I'm not sure
I'm ready to face the truth between us.

LABELS–LUNCHTIME–THE LIBRARY

I plan to sit in the library
with my notebook.

I heard a whisper of an idea
last time I was in here,
and I hope that idea
has been waiting for me
in the quiet of the room.

Jyoti sits pretending to read
at an otherwise vacant library desk.

Her signed copy of the book by The Author
is propped up like it's on display,
while her hands are moving behind it.

Inside my heavy backpack,
my own signed copy is waiting for me to read.

As I get closer,
my suspicions are confirmed.

Jyoti is tapping on her phone.

I pull out the plastic-and-metal
school chair beside Jyoti,
which isn't the only free seat in the library.
I actually wanna sit with her.

"Hey," I say nonchalantly.

"Talk of the devil!" Jyoti responds.
"You and The Twins are so cute!"
Jyoti shows me the photo T took.

I take Jyoti's phone.
I zoom in on myself:
I need to ask Granny
to redo my cane rows soon.

I hand back her phone. "Are you and T
seeing each other or are you dating?"

"You'd have to ask T. What's he said?"

"He said you were just seeing each other,"
I tell her, "but you two are always texting."

"So." Jyoti shrugs. "There's your answer."

"Well, I'm seeing a guy right now
and we don't text at all," I ponder aloud
as I pull out my sky-blue notebook
from my backpack and rummage for my pencil case.

"Why not?" Jyoti asks.

"I don't know what I'd text him.
Matt's the person I text the most,
and my other best friend Vass,
and I write a lot of things down."

I find my yellow banana-shaped pencil case
and pull out a pen, then I pause.

I don't want Jyoti reading over my shoulder.
I can't write in my notebook sitting beside her.

"Why aren't you with Matt and The Boys today?
Did you guys fall out or something?" asks Jyoti.

Is she trying to get some gossip out of me?

I set my pen on top of my closed notebook.

"I just felt like some
quiet library time today," I say.
"When I came to
meet The Author,
I remembered how much
I used to enjoy
coming to the library at lunchtimes.
I never knew you
spent lunchtimes in here, too.
I never saw you
in here in year seven and eight
when I was here almost every day."

"It's a recent thing for me," says Jyoti.

"Oh yeah?" I say inanely.

"I'm entering my literary era," says Jyoti,
pointing to the book by The Author,
which she's clearly not been reading.
"It's calmer in here than the lunch hall,
the art room, or the drama studio."

"But how will you get your gossip
if you're not out there amongst it?" I ask.

"Well, you brought the gossip to me today," she says.
"You told me voluntarily that you're seeing someone."

"Yes, I guess I did. But it's not a secret."

"Is it someone at school?" she asks, excited.

"No, he's not at this school.
He's some private-school boy I met at bouldering."

"Does this 'private-school boy' have a name?"
Jyoti copies my own glum tone.

"Obi," I offer, but say no more.

"You don't seem too excited to talk about him."

"I feel excited when I'm with him,
but when I'm not with him, I forget about him.

When I see you and T are texting all the time,
I wonder why I don't ever feel like texting Obi."
I pause to weigh my words before I continue.
"Like, I've had some stuff going on recently
and Matt's been the one to help me through it.
I didn't even think to ask Obi for his advice.
I didn't even tell Obi what's been happening."

"But you and Matt . . ." Jyoti trails off.

"Me and Matt what?"

"You're best friends."
Jyoti says this oddly,
but I don't take the bait.

"Isn't the goal supposed to be
that your romantic partner
becomes your best friend eventually?" I ask.

"No, not necessarily," says Jyoti, thinking.
"That's not always the healthiest thing.
Imagine you made your romantic partner
your everything: if you broke up
there would be nothing and no one else left.
That would be super depressing."

"So, T's not becoming your best friend?"

"Don't get me wrong, I like your cousin.
But I wouldn't go so far as to say
he's becoming my best friend.

He might not become my boyfriend.
Sometimes I think he's more lonely
than romantically interested in me.
He needs someone to listen to him.
I think he's misunderstood.
I think he's a good person."
Jyoti pauses to weigh her words.
"I think 'seeing each other'
means seeing how it goes.
It's one of those slippery labels.
It might go toward becoming a couple.
It might go toward becoming friends.
It might fade to nothing."

Mrs. James shushes us, and we obey.

"And there's this," Jyoti whispers,
and gestures to the space between us.

"What?" I ask, royally confused.

"This conversation with you.
We've not done much of this before.
If I wasn't seeing your cousin,
we wouldn't have had our little run-in
and gone from enemies to friends,
or whatever this is . . ." She trails off.

"We were never enemies," I scoff.

"I'm glad to hear that," says Jyoti.
"You do know I'm sorry

for the trouble I caused for you and Matt,
and between you and T."

"Yes, I know," I say gently.
"I've been meaning to
apologize to you as well.
I'm sorry Matt and I
were kinda rude to you
when you were trying
to set the record straight."

"Or not straight." Jyoti points at me.

I laugh too loudly.

Mrs. James shushes us again.

"I'd like us to be friends," Jyoti whispers.

"I'd like that, too," I whisper-giggle back.

I may not trust her completely,
but I'm starting to like Jyoti.

SOMETHING EPIC

MATT: Where have you been?

KAI: In the library. Do you miss me?

MATT: You wish! But you just missed something epic!

KAI: What happened?

MATT: Nathan kicked off at Kojo in the lunch hall
because Kojo said something homophobic.

KAI: Was it about me?

MATT: Not even. Kojo said something really bad about
lesbians. Nathan jumped up and started shouting, "You
know my sister's a lesbian! What's wrong with you?
You're mad if you think you can say shit like that around
me!"

KAI: What did Kojo say to that? And what did you say?

MATT: No one said anything for a few seconds. The entire

lunch hall was silent and Kojo just sat there looking at his plate. Nathan stood over him shouting at the back of his head: "I dare you to say that again and I'll box you in your mouth and knock out your teeth!"

KAI: And then what happened?

MATT: Kwesi stood up and I thought he was going to calm Nathan down, but instead, he said, "Kojo, you need to find another table."

KAI: And what did you say?

MATT: I didn't know what to say. Kojo stood up slowly and he looked at Kwesi, who was calm, then he looked at Nathan, who was breathing heavily, and I thought to myself, "They can all throw a decent punch, and this will be a madness if it kicks off."

KAI: So, what happened?

MATT: Kojo looked at the rest of us at the table. Abdi and Sam were either side of me. I folded my arms. They shook their heads. Kojo knew we weren't gonna back him.

KAI: And then?

MATT: And then Kojo looked down at the ground and just walked out, with Nathan shouting behind him, "That's right! That's what I thought! Keep walking!"

THURSDAY: ADDITIONAL SUPPORT–
LUNCHTIME–MR. NDOUR'S CLASSROOM

The door is open when I arrive,
and Ms. Sarpong waits with him.

I've spent the entire morning worrying
since my form tutor told me in morning registration
I had to come to Mr. Ndour's classroom at lunchtime.

"Come in, Malachi," says Mr. Ndour,
"and have a seat." He points
to a plastic school chair
directly in front of his desk.
He sits in his cushioned swivel chair.
I notice how he now has
a Progress Pride flag badge
pinned to his staff lanyard.

Ms. Sarpong doesn't speak.

She's seated to the left of Mr. Ndour's desk
in a regular chair like mine

but, somehow, she seems to be
the one in the driver's seat,
like Mr. Ndour is her puppet
or ventriloquist's dummy.

"How are you doing today?" Mr. Ndour asks me.

I feel like this is a trick question
and I don't know what to say.

"The reason I ask," he continues,
"is because I'm aware there's been some
division amongst your friendship group."

I feel instantly hot with anger
and the words jump out of me:
"That had nothing to do with me.
I wasn't even in the lunch hall at the time.
I was in the library with Jyoti.
                                        Ask her.
Ask The Boys.
            They'll tell you,
                        I wasn't there."

"Take a big breath, Malachi,"
Ms. Sarpong says from the sidelines.
I look at her officious smile
and then into her kind eyes.
"Mr. Ndour only asked you how you are doing;
he did not accuse you of any wrongdoing."

I take a deep breath in and out again

and I realize that it's true.
Mr. Ndour didn't say I'd caused division
but I somehow jumped to that conclusion.
I take another deep breath.

"Well done, Malachi," says Ms. Sarpong
with a warmer smile.
"Okay. Carry on," she says to Mr. Ndour.

"Malachi, I promise
I'm not accusing you of anything.
I'm just checking in,
which is my pastoral duty
as your head of year.
I'm speaking to everyone
in your group of friends
separately,
because I've realized
I need to treat you as individuals
and not lump you all in together
as I have, regrettably, done so far."

I feel like these are
Ms. Sarpong's words,
even though they come
from Mr. Ndour's mouth.
In any case it's a relief
to hear them.

"So, I'm not in trouble?" I ask, relieved.

"No, you're not in trouble," says Mr. Ndour.

"We just wanted to know
if you think you need any additional support."

"What kinda support?" I ask, confused.

"We've noticed you can be quick to anger,
and we wondered if a referral
to our school counselor would be helpful
if you wanted someone to talk to
who isn't a teacher." Mr. Ndour pauses
to weigh his words before he continues.
"Personally, I can tell you I've benefited greatly
from seeing a therapist about my own anger issues.
I could set up an initial meeting for you
with our school counselor next week,
if that's something you'd be interested in.
You don't have to decide right now
but I'll give you some information to take home.
I've already spoken to your mum
and she's on board with the idea."
Mr. Ndour pushes a pamphlet across his desk.
"Read this and discuss it with your mum
and then let me know if you want me to
go ahead and make the referral."
Mr. Ndour lets out a big breath and I wonder if
this conversation is difficult for him, too.
"Something else that may be of interest to you
is that we've invited The Author to come in next term
to do some creative writing workshops
with a select group of students, after school
in the library with Mrs. James."
He pushes more paper across his desk.

"Here's all the information about that.
I know you're hoping to be an author one day."

"Thank you, sir," I say, gathering it up
and stuffing it into my already full backpack.

I remember my anger
in the assembly hall,
when I wanted to throw
this heavy backpack
at Mr. Ndour's head,
and I think maybe
speaking to a counselor
could be a good idea.

I really love the idea
of creative writing workshops
with The Author.
I haven't had time
to read his book yet,
but my signed copy waits for me
inside my backpack.

"One last thing before I let you go."
Mr. Ndour's voice snaps
my attention back to him.
"I'm sorry if you've felt
unfairly targeted by me," he says.

"Thank you, sir," I say, astonished.

I'm shocked to get an apology from a teacher.

I think of Obi, who apologizes
for everything all the time,
to the point that his apologies
have lost their meaning
and sometimes feel annoying.
But Mr. Ndour's apology
is meaningful and overdue.

"I want the best for you, Kai.
According to all your heads of years
throughout school
you've been a model student.
You've never had
so much as an official warning,
let alone a detention,
before this academic year.
I would like to put
the past few weeks behind us:
chalk them up to experience.
As I've said, what I've learned is
I need to treat each
and every student as an individual,
regardless of who
their group of friends is.
Don't get me wrong,
that's not me saying
I think The Boys are bad news
or you shouldn't hang out with them.
I just want to remind you
not to lose your sense of self
for any group, or anyone else."

These are the words of Mr. Ndour,
I can feel it.

He cares about me.
He wants to help me.

I can admit that
I might've been wrong about him.

"I'll do my best, sir,"
I say, and I mean it.

DARK HUMOR–NIGHTTIME–
MY BEDROOM

Mum and I agree
seeing the school counselor
is a good idea for me,
and I'll sign up for
the creative writing workshops.

With that out of the way,
the next topic on my agenda
in this late-night meeting with Mum
is to ask her permission
to go to Obi's house party this Saturday.

"Matt and Vass are both allowed to go," I say,
"and Theía Estélla will pick us up
no matter how late the party goes.
But no matter how late I get back,
I promise I'll be up in time for work."

Mum looks like she wants to argue.
I think she's about to impose a curfew,

which I'm already willing to accept
as long as I can go for a few hours.

Mum opens her mouth to speak,
then closes it.

Mum shrugs, then nods.

I try out some dark humor on her.
"Can I please hear some verbal consent?"

I feel guilty when Mum doesn't smile.
"Yes, you can go to Obi's party," she says.
"I trust you to be sensible
και να προσέχεις τον Βασίλειο."

We talked about Vass's sexual assault recently,
after Theía Estélla told Mum
that Vass had told me.

Mum went to great pains
to make it clear
her previous comment
about my bad judgment
was about school,
and not anything to with
what happened to Vass.

But she went on and on
about the importance of
verbal consent, clear boundaries, and limits.

I didn't open up to Mum
about how I was feeling at the time
because it was all too confusing.
Since then, I've noticed
a combination of three main feelings
coming and going,
like tides of emotion pushing in and
ebbing away again,
with no clear boundary between them:
I've felt guilty that I let Vass go off with Adonis;
I've felt guilty about my fantasies
before I knew what he'd done to Vass;
I've felt upset that Vass isn't pressing charges; and
I've felt fear that it could be me
who is sexually assaulted
by someone similar one day.
Someone handsome, charming, and disarming.

Vass is one of the strongest
and most confident people I know.
I don't know how I'd handle
what they've been through.

SATURDAY: GREAT EXPECTATIONS—OBI'S HOUSE PARTY

I expected Obi's house party
would be more like a frat party
in an American teen movie.

I expected music to be blasting
from a massive sound system
as I stepped onto the gravel driveway
with Matt and Vass flanking me.

I expected there to be red Solo cups
and perhaps a beer pong game in play.
Instead, there's a slow record playing
on an old-school record player.

I expected Jenny to greet us enthusiastically,
since she knows all three of us,
but she waves without getting up.
She's seated in the middle of a group
of eclectically dressed individuals
on sofas and floor cushions, and

I can only assume this is The Coven.

This reminds me of Nicky Anderson's house party,
but whiter, posher, and more witchy.

To the left of Jenny and The Coven
there's a massive bookcase
the height and width of an entire wall.

I feel myself pulled toward it.

I want to read the titles
and the authors' names
on the spines of these books.
Perhaps I could
pick one to get lost in
for the whole evening.

Obi holds me back with one long arm
around me, and another around Vass.
Obi wears a Sex Pistols band T-shirt
with the words "God Save the Queen"
over the eyes of our former monarch.

"I'll give you the tour before
I introduce you to The Coven," Obi says.

"The Coven?" Matt asks
as he backs away from us.

"They're harmless," says Obi.
"No need to look so alarmed."

I give Matt a look that says *Be cool.*

"Let's have this tour," says Vass,
to break the tension between us.

"Righto, off we go," says Obi.
"This is the lounge, that's the kitchen,
and this is the guest lavatory."
Obi turns the door handle.

"*Ocupado*," says a high-pitched voice
behind the locked door.

"Sorry, Hugo," says Obi.

"No worries, Obe," says Hugo, in a deeper voice.

"Follow me," Obi says to us.

We follow Obi up the stairs:
me first, then Matt and Vass.

"Mother and Father are the top floor.
They're both out of town tonight.
My brother and I share this floor.
That's his bedroom." Obi points to a closed door.
"And we share this bathroom."

When Obi opens the bathroom door,
a hint of lavender and a steamy mirror tells me
one of them has showered recently.

"Is your brother home?" I ask Obi.

"No," says Obi, now nervous. "He's, erm,
staying with his boyfriend tonight and, erm,
speaking of which, this is my bedroom."

When Obi opens his bedroom door
I expect to see his guitar and amplifier,
posters on the wall and clothes on the floor.
But I see only a perfectly made bed,
a light brown, new-looking wooden desk
with a matching chair of the same wood,
and a mirrored built-in wardrobe
the height and width of an entire wall.
It looks like there's a mirror world.
I look into my own eyes and wonder
what might be different on the other side.

"It looks like a showroom," I say,
unable to mask my disappointment.
"And where's your guitar?" I ask.
"Do you keep it in the wardrobe?
Are you a closeted musician?"
I joke but no one gets it.
I guess it wasn't as funny
to them as it was to me.

"Wait and see," says Obi,
with a hint of mischief.
"This isn't the last stop of the tour."
He takes me by the hand.

"I always save the best for last."
He gives my hand a squeeze.
Maybe it's just in my mind,
but it seems a bit suggestive.

Obi keeps hold of my hand
and keeps smiling back at me
as we trail him downstairs
and through the kitchen,
to the far end of the garden
where there's another building.

"Welcome to the studio," says Obi proudly.

Obi points up to a green neon sign:
"This is where the magic happens."

On another wall, his band's name,
FRSH MNT T, is scrawled in lime-green
graffiti writing with a black outline.

"How do you say that?"
Matt whispers to Vass.

"Fresh Mint Tea," Vass whispers back.
"But it's giving brat," they add.
"You into Charli XCX?" they ask Obi.

"Not really," Obi answers.
"I'm more into bands than solo artists.
Here's our drum kit, keys,
guitar, bass, banjo, violin,

mandolin, trumpet, accordion."
Obi points and names it all.

I notice a stack of battered notebooks
on the green music studio sofa.
"Are these your notebooks?" I ask Obi.
I'm much more interested
in these than the instruments.

"They're the band's notebooks,"
Obi answers nonchalantly.
"We share everything here."
Obi must see the confusion
on my face, so he explains.
"It's our punk philosophy.
Anyone can play any instrument,
and we write collaboratively.
Everyone mucks in with lyrics,
melodies—everything, really."

"I can't imagine sharing my writing
with anyone but Vass," I say.
I turn to Matt and add, "No offense."

"It's cool." Matt laughs.
"You can spare me your horny poetry."

Obi looks at Matt, who smiles
mischievously at me and Vass.
No one knows how to react
to Matt's inappropriate comment,
so we collectively ignore it.

In the next room, "Mixing desk."
In the next room, "Kitchen."
In the next room, "Lavatory."

"You could pretty much
live in here," says Vass,
"and just go into the house
to sleep and shower."

"That's pretty much it," says Obi.
"I only sleep and do, erm,
homework in my bedroom."
Obi slinks an arm around me,
and pulls me in possessively.
"For now, at least," Obi says.

Matt's and Vass's eyes open wide,
like a pair of unfortunate deer
caught in our headlights.

I feel responsible for all of us
being here right now.
Technically, I was the one
who asked Obi out.

I felt embarrassed when Obi
didn't move to me confidently,
but now that he's acting confident,
I'm still embarrassed by Obi.

I expected to feel excited

in a moment like this:
Obi openly flirting with me.

I expected to feel butterflies,
but I'm drowning in
an ocean of emotion.

Obi is showing off all his stuff
and making suggestive comments
in front of my best friends.

I don't worry when Matt or Vass touch me.
I trust their hands on me.

I don't trust Obi as much.

Obi is handsome, charming, and disarming,
but I've got my guard up.

I think of what Obi is suggesting
we do in his bedroom.
I think of how lucky I felt
when I realized Obi liked me.
I think of how lucky Obi is
to have all this stuff.
I think of sitting on a swing set
with Vass at the far end
of Yiayia and Bapou's garden
while Obi was probably
in this music studio.
I think of all the time we wasted
on a sun lounger in Larnaca,

waiting for Adonis to notice Vass,
while Matt was in London
boxing with The Boys.
I think of Vass being
sexually assaulted by Adonis,
and how Vass didn't tell me
until weeks later.
I think of Adonis's expectant smile
when he turned to me.

"And you are?" Adonis asked me.

I think of the possibility
of Adonis sexually assaulting me
and not Vass.

And then I think of me and Obi
naked in front of his mirrored wardrobe,
and what might be different on the other side.

I expected to feel butterflies,
but a tidal wave of anger takes me over.

"Obi, can you just chill out?"
I blurt as I shrug him off.

From the stunned silence I know
I'm the one who needs to chill.

Matt gives *me* the *Be cool* look.

I don't know what to say or where to look.

I don't know what about Obi puts me off:
if it's his privilege or suggestive comments
in front of my best friends.

Matt—who I still fancy.
Vass—who was sexually assaulted recently.

It's too much for me
to deep it all at once.

Obi reaches for the jade pendant around his neck.
He rubs it between his thumb and index finger,
like a voice inside that green stone
will tell him what to say next.

"Erm, I'm sorry, Kai." Obi apologizes
for what feels like the millionth time,
like a broken record or a boring song.

I remember Mr. Ndour's classroom
and Ms. Sarpong reminding me to breathe.
I take a deep breath in and out again.

"Don't worry. It's fine," I lie.
"Can we go back into the house
and meet your friends?" I ask.

THE DEVIL YOU KNOW

MATT: I'm home.

KAI: Thanks for letting me know.
I wish you would've let us call Vass's mum to pick you up.

MATT: It's all good. I couldn't have her come just for me.
Are you staying there much longer?

KAI: Yes, I think so. Vass is having fun.
Obi and I are just chilling.

MATT: Cool. Enjoy the rest of your night then.
And try not to communicate with any demons.

KAI: It's too late for that. I'm already talking to you!

MATT: 😺 Do you think you and Obi will have sex
tonight?

KAI: No, not tonight.

MATT: You sure? He was all over you before.

KAI: Yes, I'm sure. Why? Is that the real reason you left?
You jealous? 😙

MATT: You wish I was jealous! 😌 No, it was the tarot
cards, like I said.
They freaked me out. Especially the one with the devil on.
That's definitely against my religion.

KAI: What about being gay? And how is the devil on a
tarot card any different from the devil emoji? 😈

MATT: I don't know. It just is. No offense to SG and Obi's
friends but there's something off-key about them. If it
looks like a coven, calls itself a coven, and does spooky
shit like a coven, then it's probably a coven. 🕷 👻 🧹

KAI: I see what you're saying. They're different to the
people you're used to, but I think they're harmless, like
Obi says. We get lots of customers like them on Mum's
market stall.

MATT: Ah! I see how it is now. You're trying to drum up
business for your mum's stall? 😬

KAI: 🔮 I might have mentioned it. Two of them said
they'd come by tomorrow. 🔮 🔮

MATT: But you're not in the market for Obi's dick tonight? 🤏 😼

KAI: 💀 Bye!

MATT: 👻

LATER THAT NIGHT: THE DEVIL YOU DON'T KNOW–OBI'S HOUSE PARTY

"Matt's home now," I tell Obi.

"That's good," says Obi,
looking up at me with a forced smile.

I don't understand why
Obi is sitting on the floor,
leaning against my legs,
while I'm sitting by myself
on this two-seater sofa.

Vass is chatting happily
with Jenny and The Coven,
but it feels like Obi and I
are waiting for something.

When Obi's smile fades,
I feel compelled to reach down
and stroke his face,
like he's a moping puppy.

"What's wrong, Obi?" I ask
in a hushed tone,
even though I think I know.

"I just wanted your pals
to like mine," Obi whispers.

"Vass seems to be enjoying themselves,"
I tell Obi, nodding my head toward Vass.

They're getting on with The Coven
like a house on fire,
which is what this might be
if they knock over
the candles they're lighting.

"What are they doing now?
Are they casting a spell?"
I ask Obi, to change the subject
and lighten the mood.

"I don't know," Obi sulks.
He crosses his arms with a childish shrug.
He's disappointed
I've changed the subject.

I decide to tell him what I'm thinking.

"Listen, Obi," I whisper, quieter than before.
"Here's the tea: Matt's a bit of a hypocrite
when it comes to his religion.

He uses it as an excuse to avoid things
and get out of certain situations.
He picks and chooses what matters to him.
It's not for me to judge him
but, as you can hear, I struggle not to.
I wanted Matt to get on with your friends, too.
But Matt's not someone I can have
any fixed expectations of.
If Matt and I are gonna stay friends,
I have to try to love and accept him
for all his contradictions."

I let out a sigh and lean back into the sofa.
I never thought I'd feel such sweet relief
from spilling the tea to Obi, of all people.

Obi rises from the floor
and sits beside me.
He nuzzles into my shoulder.
He smells of lavender.
I breathe him in deeply.
A breath of fresh air.
For the first time since I got here,
I feel calm. I feel cozy.

"Thank you for sharing that,"
Obi says, his voice full of breath.
He nuzzles into my shoulder
for a moment longer, before
he sits up and speaks quietly:
"I agree with everything you said.
The Coven's into all this

but, just between me and you,
I couldn't care less about any of it.
Hugo goes along with it
because he's Jenny's boyfriend.
Jenny's my best bud, but
The Coven is her thing, not mine.
They bring their booze, tarot cards,
candles, and stuff for their spells.
My house became their covenstead
because the 'rents are rarely here.
Other than Jenny, my only friends
are my big brother and our band.
I don't get to hang out with my brother
as much since he got a boyfriend."
Wide-eyed inspiration
illuminates Obi's face.
"Maybe we could
go on a double date with them?
Maybe you could
come watch our band practice?
Maybe you could
write us some song lyrics?"

Obi speaks so brightly it dazzles me.

I feel guilty.
My feelings don't match his.

"Maybe," I say, taking in all this
information, and all these possibilities.

Obi rubs the jade pendant between

his thumb and index finger once again.
His body beside mine now
feels like a surrender compared to earlier,
when he gripped me possessively.

I touch the evil eye bracelet
around my left wrist,
from Mum.

"Let's go to my bedroom." Obi smiles
with a flash of his fangs,
as Vass would call them.

I feel like Red Riding Hood,
but instead of Granny's house in the woods,
I've willingly gone to the den
of the Big Bad Wolf.

Obi clearly isn't a bad person, says my angel.

He could be a wolf in sheep's clothing, says my devil.

I look over at Vass, Jenny, and The Coven,
who are now holding hands
and chanting something.

"Why do you wanna go to your bedroom?" I ask.

"To kiss you," Obi says, smiling again,
and leaning his body into mine.

"You can kiss me here,"

I say, in a low-key panic,
knowing I'm not ready
to do anything more than kiss.

"I'd prefer to do it in private," he says.
"You know, I've been dying to get you alone
from the moment I met you."

I don't feel I can trust myself
or Obi if I'm not clear, here
and now, before we go upstairs.

I remember what Mum said
about verbal consent,
boundaries, and limits.
"Just kissing and nothing more."

"Of course," says Obi, sitting upright.

"Have I offended you?" I ask.

"No," Obi says forcefully.

I can feel he's about to get sulky.

I feel guilty.
Maybe I led him on.

I did come on strong
with my flirting
in the restaurant.

I haven't told him I'm a virgin.

"You know I like you," I say.
"But I'm not in a rush
to go all the way.
Not tonight, anyway."

Obi lets out a long sigh.
"Okay," he says.
He stands and offers a hand.
"Just kissing. Nothing more."

It feels like when someone haggles
for a better deal on Mum's market stall.

Verbal consent,
boundaries, and limits
doesn't feel as romantic
as I expected,
but going upstairs
doesn't feel scary anymore.

I take Obi's hand
and rise from the sofa.

I look over at Vass again,
and they look my way.

They mouth the words, *Are you okay?*

I smile and nod because I am.

I'm not sure what I'm feeling,
but it's not bad anymore.

I'm going upstairs
to kiss a hot boy
who wants me
to go on double dates
and write lyrics
for his folk punk band.

He's something different.
He's a breath of fresh air.

I lift Obi's hand in mine.

Vass smiles and nods. They understand.

I turn to Obi. "Okay," I say,
"let's go to your bedroom."

SUNDAY: MORE THAN FRIENDS-MUM'S MARKET STALL

"You're making it sound so weird,"
I whisper to Matt, covering my face
and feeling my flushed cheeks.

"That's because it is weird," Matt whispers back.
"You were locking lips with Obi upstairs,
with a satanic ritual going on downstairs."

"Maybe, but you don't have to say it like that,"
I protest through gritted teeth.

Matt's wearing his church clothes.
If Mum gets back with our breakfast baps
before Matt has to go, I know she'll go on
about how handsome Matt looks.

Matt grips the lapels of his blazer.
He stands upright and looks down at me.
All of a sudden, he looks like a Big Man,
and I know what he's about to do.

He's about to become Pastor Matthew.
"What shall become of you,
         Malachi Michaelides?"

I crease over with laughter
and when I recover, I look up at Matt.
"Is that you, Pastor Matthew?"

"Yes, my son,
         and I want you
to fully comprehend
         the magnitude
of your situation
         and assess
your life choices," he says.

"I just can't with Pastor Matthew today,"
I say, covering my eyes with my hands.

"You know I'm joking,
don't you?" says Matt.
"I'm happy for you, my little devil."

"Of course I know you're joking,"
I say, uncovering my eyes
and facing Matt's handsomeness.

There's a hint of mischief in his eyes.
"I've thought of a story idea for you.
Wanna hear it?"

"Go on," I say, giving a green light

to whatever foolishness
is about to come out
of Matt's magnificent mouth.

I'm excited. I'm turned on
by Matt's playful energy right now.

I feel like kissing Obi
has awoken something in me.

We did a little more than kiss.
We got a little handsy.
I felt Obi's swimmer's physique:
rock-hard six-pack abs
under his Sex Pistols band T-shirt.

I can imagine kissing Matt.
His bulging boxer's biceps
holding me ever so tightly.

"Here's my idea," Matt says.
"Obi targeted you to bring you to The Coven
because they needed a virgin
for their demonic satanic pagan virgin blood ritual."

"Did you practice saying that?" I ask.

"Yes, I did." Matt smiles and nods.

"Demonic, satanic, and pagan
are three different things." I laugh.

"You'd know, wouldn't you?"
Matt tilts his head and tuts three times.
The morning sun makes a marvel
of Matt's jawline.

I feel a lump in my throat.
I cough it clear.

"Let's go back to your story idea.
Since I'm still a virgin,
this could go one of two ways
when I see them again:
The Coven could sacrifice me
in a 'demonic satanic pagan virgin blood ritual,'
just like you said,
or I could lose my virginity to Obi,
join The Coven,
and bring them a replacement virgin."
I point at Matt and tilt my head,
because I know he is.

Matt coughs and turns into
Pastor Matthew again:
"Or you could accept
          Jesus
as your Lord and savior and
          rebuke
those pagan demons!"

I crease over with laughter again.

"Oh my God, Matt! Look at you!"

Mum shrieks as she hands me
two white paper bags:
our vegan sausage baps.
She throws her arms up
and around Matt.

"Hello, Auntie, how are you?"
Matt says, bent into a hug with Mum.

"I'm great!" says Mum. "How are you?"
She releases Matt and takes a step back.

"I'm good, Auntie."
Matt smiles goofily,
on best behavior.
"I just came by to say hi to Kai
on my way to church."

Matt's Church Boy act is impeccable.

Mum looks up at Matt dreamily
before she turns to me.
"Isn't Matt so sweet?
Doesn't he look so handsome
and muscular in his suit?"

Matt looks embarrassed,
effervescently,
like he loves and hates this
in equal measure.

"Absolutely dreamy!"

I agree with Mum.
I pile on the compliments:
"Stunning! Gorgeous!
Tens across the board!"

"I'd better get going,"
Matt says, laughing.
"I'll text you later, okay?"

"Okay," I say, realizing
I feel a little flushed.

"It's nice to see you, Auntie."
Matt waves at Mum.

"It's nice to see you, too."
Mum waves back at Matt.

As Matt turns away, I notice
the curve of his buttocks
and the outline of the afro comb
in his back right pocket.

As we watch Matt walk away,
I hand Mum the white paper bag
with her breakfast bap inside.

Both of our bags crinkle with every bite
as we begin to munch on their contents.

Mum nudges me gently with her elbow
and speaks with a muffled mouthful.

"Didn't you go with Matt and Vass
to Obi's party last night?" she asks.

"Yes," I say, my mouth full, too.
I chew and clear my throat again. "Why?"

"You see Matt every weekday at school.
You go bouldering together on Saturdays.
You went to a party together last night.
He's popped by to see you this morning.
And he's gonna text you later . . ." Mum waits.

While Mum's logic is flawless,
she's stacking a house of cards
I have long since given up on.
"What are you saying, Mum?"

"I guess I was wondering
        if you and Matt were
                more than friends?"

"Of course
        Matt and I are
                more than friends."

My answer is intentionally mischievous.

Mum turns toward me
with wide-eyed wonder.

        "Matt and I are
                the best of friends."

"So, you're not . . . ?" She stops there.

"No, Mum." I chuckle.
"I thought you'd already guessed.
I'm seeing Obi," I say.

Mum is jolted by this.

"Oh,
        Obi.
                Of course, you're seeing Obi."

Mum processes this news,
and the trick I played on her
with my surprise turn.

I take a satisfied bite
of my breakfast bap.

"I couldn't tell if Obi was gay,"
Mum says casually,
"because he's just so posh."

I splutter and spray the ground
with bits of bread and vegan sausage.
"Mum! I can't believe you said that!"

"We're still allowed to call posh people
'posh,' aren't we?" Mum asks in earnest.

I shrug, teasing Mum again.

"Come off it, Kai.
You know what I mean . . . ?"

I know what she means,
but I shrug once again.

Now Mum can't tell
if I'm joking or not.

"Obi seems lovely."
Mum places a hand on my arm.
"But we've known Matt for longer.
So, I've had longer to wonder
about you and Matt.
But no, it's not you and Matt.
It's you and Obi."
Mum squeezes my arm gently.
"And you're happy?"

"Yes, I'm happy!" I smile and nod.

Mum pulls me into a tight squeeze.
"Well, if you're happy,
I'm happy," she says.

I hear a crinkling by my ear,
as Mum takes another bite
of her breakfast bap
over my shoulder.

THE FOLLOWING SATURDAY: BEFORE A FALL–
BOULDERING

"Μπράβο, αγάπη μου,"
Vass cheers up at me from the crash mat,
as I reach the top hold
of a difficult problem,
only just within my arm's length.
"Smile for the camera," they say.

As I release one hand to turn
and give Vass a thumbs-up for the photo,
my other hand loses its grip.

In an instant I see Vass's eyes change
from proud to afraid.

I recall a Bible verse
I heard at Matt's church,
something about pride
coming before a fall.

This doesn't feel like flight.

It's my inevitable downfall.

I can't remember how Coach said
we were supposed to fall.

My eyes drop from Vass's face
to the crash mat rushing toward me.

There's nothing to keep me
suspended in the air,
no hands at my waist,
like I did for Olivia
on the monkey bars.

This descent has been
a lifetime in the making.

I hear Granny's voice say:
        "You're supposed to be
        the good one, Malachi,"
and I feel myself flail
and twist
into an improbable position.

My right foot and elbow
are the first parts of my body
to make impact.

I'm flat on my back on the crash mat.

For a moment I can't feel anything
and then a tingle builds in my body,

like a surge of electricity,
like the most extreme version
of pins and needles you can imagine.
I want my mum.

Through the cloud of chalk
thrown up by my impact
with the crash mat,

I see Matt and Vass are to one side of

        me,

and Jenny and Obi are to the other.

"Don't move!" Superhero Jenny tells me.

I think of how Jenny jumps from the wall,
even though we're not supposed to,
but Jenny's never fallen or injured herself.

The others look as helpless
and shook as I feel.

"Don't touch him!"
Jenny says to them.
"I'll get Coach."

Vass starts crying. "It's my fault
for making him pose for a photo."

I try my best to sit up,

to reassure Vass that this wasn't their fault.
Only then do I feel
the most intense pain in my ankle and elbow
and yell out in agony.

Coach returns with Jenny
and tells everyone
to move away from me.

I'm sitting up. I cup my right elbow
with my left hand.
I can't stand without support,
so Coach lets Vass
come with us to the hospital.

I feel like Skellig, carried
from the junk-filled garage
to the abandoned house
with a nest of fledgling owls in the attic.

I don't have wings, and I'll never fly.

Theía Estélla meets us
and takes over from Coach
as my guardian.
Theía Estélla is an angel,
but I still want my mum.

After my X-rays, the doctor says
neither my ankle nor my elbow
seems to be fractured.

They say I can take painkillers.
I can't go back to bouldering
or do any high-impact activities
for six to eight weeks
or until the pain stops.

I'm sent home
with Theía Estélla (and Vass)
with a walking boot to support my foot,
and a sling to support my arm,
but all I want is my mum.

SUNDAY: THE BEST MEDICINE–MORNING–VASS'S BEDROOM

I wore one of Vass's old T-shirts to bed
with the word "OBEY" printed across the chest.

I asked to wear
their "I Can't Even Think Straight" T-shirt,
but Vass said it was too good
for sleeping in.

I slept here last night
because Mum said it would be "silly"
to move me "back and forth"
since Theía Estélla agreed to look after me today
while Mum's at her market stall.

I'm trying not to mind, but it hurts my feelings
that Mum wouldn't take a day off to take care of me:
my injured body feels like an inconvenience
that Mum doesn't want to be lumbered with.

I feel like a sack of shit

sprinkled with the rainbow glitter of
Vass and Theía Estélla's love.

I'm propped up in Vass's bed
with many heavenly pillows
behind my back and head,
a large stack of colorful cushions
under my right arm,
and a few under my right foot.

Half my limbs are out of action,
but I'm lucky I'm left-handed, I think,
as I look to the evil eye bracelet
around my left wrist.

Beside my phone, notebook, and pencil case,
a book called *Trans Teen Zine Volume One*
by a Scottish author and actor called Finlay
sits atop a stack of other books
Vass has thoughtfully gathered
for me to read in bed this morning.

They've been bringing me things,
like I'm a fledgling in their nest,
kinda like Michael does for Skellig.

I'm lucky to have Vass, I think.

"You have a visitor, sir,"
Vass announces formally,
like they're my servant.
Their long hair is all pinned up

like a maid or a matron.

"How's the patient doing?"
A massive bouquet of sunflowers,
orange lilies, and orange roses,
followed by the bright white smile
of a grinning Obi,
appear around the open bedroom door.

Obi steps into the gaze
of the evil eye hanging above the door.

He wears a pink Sex Pistols band T-shirt
that I've not seen him in before.
It has the words "NO FUTURE"
in yellow capital letters across his chest.

"I'm sore," I tell Obi melodramatically,
with a random hand flourish.
"Physically and emotionally," I add.
"Mother dearest abandoned me here."
I'm play-sulking but only half joking.

I know we need the money.
I know it takes a village to raise a child,
and I'm being taken care of.
But I still want my mum.

"Η μαμά σου ήταν εδώ χθες,"
Vass says in Mum's defense.
"And haven't I been
looking after you, αγάπη μου?

I gave you my bed
and slept on the floor."
They point down to
their thin pillow and blanket.

"Yes," I say, embarrassed.
"Είσαι τέλεια, αγάπη μου," I tell Vass,
before reaching out to Obi.

He hands me the flowers
and they're heavier than I expected.

I place them on the bed beside me.

I feel crowded by the orange and yellow flowers
next to my phone, notebook, pencil case,
and the stack of Vass's books.

"I feel like John Keats," I say,
"convalescing in Rome."

A bemused Vass squints
and tilts their head at me.

An unreadable Obi
surveys the bedroom, silently.

Obi looks
dog-eared,
like the corner
of a page
folded down,

on a book
you meant to
come back to
but realize
you've lost all
interest in.

I remember

        Matt's hand on my shoulder:
        Kai, come back.

Matt's the one
I come back to.

"Who's this?" Obi points to a poster
of Vass's favorite drag performer.

"That's The Black Flamingo,"
Vass says, then smiles at me.

"They're amazing!" I tell Obi.
"They're the same mix as me."

Obi steps closer to the poster
of The Black Flamingo standing on one leg
with the other leg kicked back behind them.
They wear black high heels,
a black tutu, and a black feathered top;
they have cropped hair,
and a bright white smile
between bright red lips.

"So, they're Greek Cypriot and Jamaican, too?
I'd never heard of that mix before I met you."

Vass turns to me and says,
"Oh my! Kai! You're such an uncut gem."

I repeat the viral phrase "Uncut jaaaahms"
several times, in my best Julia Fox impression.

"You're such a Julia!" Vass points at me.

"No, you are!" I reply to them.

Both of us burst into hysterics,
but Obi doesn't get it.

Even though I'm grateful Obi has come to see me,
I already feel ready for him to leave.

I hold the flowers out to Vass.
"Will you put these in water, please?"

"Certainly, sir, much obliged,"
they say, like a servant again,
as they take the flowers off my hands.
"Anything else I can do for you, sir?"

"That'll be all, Matron," I say,
in a posh-person impression,
playing along with their game.
"Righto, cheerio, off you go,"
I add before the penny drops,

and I realize I sound like Obi.

Vass and I both look at him.

Obi looks down at Vass's pillow and blanket.
"Righto, I think I'd better go."

My cheeks burn with embarrassment.
It's my turn to be the apologetic one.

"Obi, I'm so, so sorry," I say.
"We weren't making fun of you."

I reach out my left hand for Obi,
but he's farther than arm's length.

If Obi reached out
or stepped toward me,
we could touch.
But he doesn't reach
or step my way.

Obi looks at my hand
but doesn't look me in the eye.

I look up at the evil eye hanging
above Vass's bedroom door.
I look down at the evil eye bracelet
around my left wrist.
I rest my hand back on the bed.

"Honestly, it's fine if you were,"

Obi says, keeping his distance.

"But we weren't," Vass protests.

"For goodness' sake!" Obi yells,
"I can handle a bit of banter."

Obi can't handle it.
Obi can't handle us.

Vass smiles but it doesn't reach their eyes.
Vass's smile tells Obi that he's on thin ice.

"Shit! I'm sorry."
Obi flashes his fangs, and he forces a laugh.
"Laughter is the best medicine.
At least, that's what they say.
Anyway, I have band practice.
So, I should be heading home."

Obi looks to me for permission to leave,
like a vampire who needs permission to enter.

I realize, Obi couldn't get inside,
because my heart was already occupied.

"You probably need to rest,
don't you?" Obi asks me pleadingly.

I know I should protest more,
for Obi's sake, to make sure he knows
I wasn't making fun of him.

But, like an energy vampire,
Obi has drained me
of all good feeling for him.

I don't protest. I let him go.

"You're right," I say,   wanting him
and my embarrassment   to go away,
as much as Obi wants   to leave.
"I probably do need   to rest."

I'm confused when
Obi doesn't budge,
like he's stuck in the mud.
"Erm, so, how long
before you're back
at bouldering?" he asks.

"The doctor said six to eight weeks," I reply.

"Two months?" Obi seems shocked.

"Yes, possibly," I say,
then offer, "but if Coach lets me,
I'll come as a spectator
and live vicariously through all of you.
You know, I'm not actually bedbound,
even though I look like I am right now.
I'm gonna go to school on Monday
wearing my boot and sling."

I make to point to them, but I remember
I don't know where Vass put them.
"Where are they?" I ask. "Never mind," I say,
quicker than Vass can respond.
"Last night I managed to hop along
to the toilet by myself
while Vass was asleep on the floor."

"I have a confession to make . . ."
Vass makes the sign of the cross.
"I woke up as soon as your foot hit the floor
but I enjoyed your hopping so much
I decided to leave you to it.
You were doing an amazing
Black Flamingo impression."

With the flowers in their hand,
Vass copies the pose
of The Black Flamingo in the poster.
Vass bursts out laughing,
and I can't help but join them
despite the pain in my elbow as I laugh.

"I'll let myself out," says Obi.

"See you at bouldering," says Vass,
striking the one-legged pose again.

My laughter is irrepressibly painful,
for me and perhaps for Obi as well.

"I'll text you, shall I?" Obi asks me.

"Yes, text me," I say,
gasping to catch my breath.

"Thanks for the flowers."
I squeeze out the words
through laughter and happy tears
as Obi disappears
around Vass's bedroom door.

Vass hands me a tissue
from the box on their desk.
I dry my eyes with it.

And when I hear the front door open
and close behind Obi,
everything clicks into place for me.

I remember
                    Matt telling me:
                    Real life is messy,
                    it doesn't always make sense.
                    Real life isn't a story with
                    symmetry
                    and a satisfactory
                    ending.

Things with Obi are far from satisfactory.

T and Jyoti told me
seeing each other means
seeing how it goes.

It's not been going well.
It's not the dream it was.

Obi is fresh-from-the-oven hot,
but something about him
leaves me feeling cold,
and that's not his fault.

They're not red flags, as such.
It's not a crime to be posh,
privileged, or to show off.
It's not a crime to apologize
for yourself all the time.
It's not a crime to be anxious,
if that's what Obi is.
But I find these things annoying,
and I'm easily annoyed.

I've been thinking it, but
I need to say it out loud.

"I don't wanna be with Obi," I tell Vass.
"I want to be with Matt."

They roll their eyes and tut.
"Well, that's extremely obvious."

"Is it? Is it extremely obvious?"
I mock Vass's mocking of me.

"Whatever, girl!" Vass laughs,
walking off with the flowers.

"I'll go put these in water,"
they say, over their shoulder.
"Text Matt. Invite him over."

"Vass, wait!" I say.

They come back to me.
They cradle the flowers.
They reminded me
of the goddess Persephone,
returning to earth
from the Underworld.

"Thank you for looking after me," I say,
with more tears of gratitude in my eyes.
"I know it's not the same thing,
but I wanna look after you, too.
But I don't always know what to say or do."

"Είναι εντάξει," says Vass.
"Είναι ωραία, αγάπη.
I've got my mum.
I've got my support group.
It's not all on you.
You don't have to
say or do anything different.
I want our friendship
to carry on as normal.
You're the best friend
I could ever wish for."

EMPTY-HANDED—LUNCHTIME—VASS'S BEDROOM

When Matt arrives empty-handed
in his handsome church clothes,
I'm so much more excited to see him
than I was to see Obi this morning.

The bouquet of flowers from Obi
trumpet orange and yellow beside me
from a vase on Vass's bedside table.
I pray Matt doesn't mention them.

"You look busted!" Matt says.
"How many colors is that bruise?"

"I decided I wanted to match Vass's bedroom
with a rainbow and some evil-eye blue."

Matt takes in the colors of Vass's bedroom.
He looks at my arm again,
and lets out a laugh.

I love Matt's laugh.

I think of what Obi said:
        Laughter is the best medicine.

Matt thinks of something:
"That has to be the most mixed-race bruise
I've ever seen.
You can never make your mind up
what color you wanna be."

I'm dead. Buried. A ghost.

"Matthew! How dare you?!" I howl.

We both take a moment to recover.

Still catching his breath,
Matt says, "Vass said to tell you
they're helping their mum make lunch."

He regards the big, showy flowers.

"Are you staying for lunch?" I ask.

"Auntie Estélla insisted," Matt says
as he returns his attention to me.
"You know how aunties love me,"
he says with mock-cockiness,
before he becomes more earnest.
"Is that okay with you?" he asks.

"Yes, you have to stay," I say.
"Theía Estélla is making my favorite:
μακαρόνια του φούρνου.
It's a pasta bake, like lasagna."

"Isn't fish and chips your favorite?"
Matt asks, confused.

"I meant my favorite thing
that Theía Estélla makes."

"Oh, okay," Matt says, oddly.

"What's up?" I ask, suspicious.

"Nothing's up," Matt says
as he carefully collects
the stack of Vass's books,
my phone, notebook, and pencil case,
and places them on the floor.

"Don't you need these?" he says,
picking up my boot and sling.

"I think Vass is trying to
hold me hostage here," I joke.
"Are you here to break me free?"

He chuckles. "I'm here for
whatever you need me for."
He sits beside me on the bed,
cradling the boot and sling,

one in each arm, like two babies.

He looks like a grown man.
He looks like a dad.
It's so beautiful it hurts.

"Put them down," I say, and he obeys.

I thought seeing Matt in his church clothes
in Vass's bedroom full of LGBTQ+ rainbows
would feel like a contradiction,
but it's more like an expansion
of everything I've been thinking.

By learning to accept Matt's contradictions,
there's more possibility,
and less binary thinking.

"How was church?" I ask him.
Followed by, "Did you say a little prayer for me?"

"I did, actually," Matt says gently.
Followed by: "For a quick recovery."

I want to get back
to laughing and joking with Matt.

He looks at me
like I'm a fragile little bird
with broken wings.

I look at him

like he might also have hollow bird bones
and I could lift him with one arm.

He is as delicate a creature as me.

"Did you pray for my soul as well?" I smirk.

"I think it's a bit late for that," he jokes back.

I breathe a sigh of relief.

We sit in silence for a while.

I feel as comfortable as I can,
given my injuries and the predicament I'm in.

"You know," I begin,
"when I was falling,
I thought of a Bible verse
I heard at your church."

"Oh yeah?" asks Matt.
"Which one?"

"Proverbs 16:18," I say, having looked it up
in preparation for this conversation.

"That's deep," says Matt.

"Thank God for crash mats," I joke again.

Matt looks serious.

"I'm sorry I froze when
you fell from the wall."

"It's okay," I say.
I try to lighten the mood once again:
"Spider Girl swung in and saved the day!"

"And I was useless," says Matt.

"Well, it wasn't your responsibility," I say.
Then I ask, "Do you reckon I could
sue Coach for not supervising me properly?"

A jokey tone for a few seconds:
"Yeah, I reckon you could."
Then Matt's seriousness descends.
"I know it's not Coach's fault you fell,
but he wasn't looking out for you, Kai.
He never looks out for us.
I don't know, man. It pisses me off.
His work ethic is so slack."

"I was saying exactly that
to Vass last night," I reply,
"when they were blaming
themselves for my fall.
It was obviously my own
fault for being careless,
showing off and posing
like that for Vass's photo.
But Coach lets us get away
with that kinda stuff.

He's not like Mr. Ndour,
who's always on our backs.
I have to admit." I point
to my rainbow-bruised elbow.
"This makes me appreciate
the stricter adults in my life."

I recall Mr. Ndour's advice
     "not to lose your sense of self
        for any group, or anyone else."

"Our boxing coach,
TJ, is so strict,"
Matt says dreamily,
in his own world:
the boxing gym
I've never been to.

"Oh yeah?" I ask, intrigued.

"Yeah," Matt says.
"TJ inspects our hand wraps
after we've done them,
and if he thinks
they're not good enough
he'll unravel them
and make us start again."

"I know all those words
individually," I admit,
"but I still have no idea
what you just said."

Matt laughs.
"I'll show you," he says.

He takes out his phone
and shows me a video
of how you wrap your hand
with a long strip of fabric
before you put on a boxing glove.

Afterward, Matt says,
"I'd really like you
to come to boxing
when your arm is better."

"Don't forget about my foot," I say.
I point to my rainbow-bruised ankle
elevated by colorful cushions.

"How badly does it hurt?" Matt asks,
as he lightly pokes it and I wince.

He doesn't apologize and I'm relieved.

"Probably as bad as being punched in the face."
I ball my fist, but Matt doesn't flinch.
"Has that happened to you yet?" I ask.

"No. We punch the punching bags, not each other.
We haven't started sparring yet.
We do lots of conditioning work,
like push-ups, sit-ups, and skipping."

I fail to suppress my laughter.
"Skipping?" I splutter.
"Are you telling me
you and The Boys spent the summer
skipping together?"
I laugh freely and pay the price
with the pain in my arm.
I wince again.

"Yeah, that's right." Matt smiles.

"But Nathan said you were a beast.
And Kwesi said he was scared
to be paired with you."

"That was just to hold
the punching bag in place.
I guess he could feel
my punch through the bag,
but I've not actually
punched anyone."

"Let's keep it that way," I say.

"I thought you said
I'd have to punch someone."

"When and why would I say that?"

"It was our second day back after summer.
It wasn't Pavlov's dog or Schrödinger's cat,

but it was something like that."

"Chekhov's gun . . ." I remember.

"Yeah, that was it!" Matt laughs.

He makes gun fingers.
He points them at my right foot and elbow.

"Pow!

Pow!"

I laugh a little until
I recall something else.

"But I remember you said
Nathan, Kwesi, and Kojo
could all throw a punch."

"Yeah, into the punching bag.
Come see for yourself sometime," he says.
"It might be a good outlet
for that temper of yours."

I feel embarrassed by this.
Everyone around me thinks
I have an anger problem.

I brush it off with a joke.
I repeat what Mum said:
"Every weekday at school.
Bouldering on Saturdays.

Surely you see enough of me already?"

"I could never see enough of you," Matt says,
and I can't tell if he's joking or not.

I examine Matt's serious-looking face,
and wait for him to crack a smile.

I see tears welling in his eyes.

"What's up?" I ask again.

"I was so scared when you fell . . ."
Matt starts to sob.

I reach out my left arm
and Matt falls onto the left side of my chest
and I hold him in a half embrace.

I slowly rub Matt's back with my left hand.
I bear the pain in my right elbow
caused by Matt's muscular weight
as his heavy sobs shake me.

"I'm okay," I say to my favorite boy.

It's the first time I've seen Matt cry.

I think of Granny comforting me,
and how I comforted Vass.

I was a shoulder to cry on for Vass,

and I'm a chest to sob into for Matt.

"I'm okay," I say again.

"I know," Matt mumbles into my chest.
"But what if something worse had happened."

"But it didn't. It's not that bad," I say softly.

"I love you so much," Matt sobs at my heart.

"I love you, too," I whisper,
just loud enough for him to hear.

I realize this is the first time
we've said these words
to each other in a serious way.

I realize I'm crying, too.
I can see my used tissue on the bed
but I don't have a free hand
to reach out for it.

My tears flow
down my cheeks
and fall
into Matt's afro.

"I'm getting tears in your hair."
I giggle through my waterworks.
I continue to rub Matt's back.

The fist-shaped handle
of Matt's afro comb is half out
of his back right pocket.

"I don't care," Matt mumbles into my chest again.
"I don't know what I'd do without you."

I laugh.

"Come on, Matt."

I pickpocket Matt's afro comb.

I wait for a reaction
but it doesn't come.

I poke his ribs with its metal tines.

No reaction. Nothing at all.

"Come on, Matt," I repeat.
"You don't have to worry.
I'm not on my deathbed.
I'm just a bit battered and bruised."

Matt sits up slowly
with a stern look on his face
that becomes more pleading
with each passing second.

Matt wants me to read his mind,
but I've given up trying.

I wipe my eyes with my used tissue.

"There's a box of tissues
on the desk," I say.

He doesn't break eye contact.
His face isn't as wet as I'd expect.

His tears are on my chest.

There's a wet patch
on the left side of my chest,
right over my heart
and the "Y" of "OBEY."

Why Obi?

Because I didn't think
Matt liked me back.

We stare at each other.
We both breathe heavily.

When I venture a smile,
Matt smiles back at me.

I can feel what Matt wants to say
because I wanna say it, too.

I want Matt
                to say it first.

I need Matt
                to say it first.

Matt gulps
and swallows before
he speaks,
like he's had
a mouthful
of rainbow sprinkles.

"Remember when we were watching
Nicky Anderson and her girlfriend?"

"Yes, of course I remember," I say.

"Do you remember what I said?" Matt asks me.

"'I want that one day,'" I answer.

"That's right," Matt says, "and then you said,
'I want that, too,' didn't you?"

"Something like that," I say casually,
even though my heart is racing.

"I've thought about it a lot," says Matt.

"Oh yeah?" I ask, fake-casual again.

"Yeah . . ." He trails off.
He shakes his head
and narrows his eyes,

disappointed in me
for not taking the bait,
or in himself for taking so long
to get to the point.

"Have you come to a conclusion?"
I ask, to help him along.

He weighs his words before he speaks.
"When I said, 'I want that one day,'
the person I saw myself with was you."

That's what I've been waiting to hear,
but it doesn't feel like enough.

"What do you see now?" I ask.

"I see you, Kai. Only you," Matt says.
"I know you're seeing Obi.
I know it's selfish of me to tell you now.
But you're the person I see myself with."
He weighs his words once more.
"You know, in the future, when I'm out."

I wince because it feels like
I've been punched in the gut.

Matt's words wind me worse
than my crash landing yesterday.

This dream is unraveling.

Matt's only talking
about this hypothetically, isn't he?

Pathetic! says my devil.

Matt sees himself with me
in a hypothetical future,
when he's ready to come out.
Years from now when he's out
of his parents' house
at a faraway university.

That may be Matt's story,
but it's not mine.

My devil takes hold,
and my rage jumps out:
"Fuck off, Matt!
You're not doing this to me."

"What do you mean?"
Matt asks as he sits up.
He shuffles back on the bed.

"You're not gonna dangle
some fantasy in front of me
of us being together,
years into the future,
when you're ready to come out."

"Kai, please wait," he says.
He puts a hand on my left leg.

"You haven't let me finish.
Just let me finish."
He squeezes gently.
He looks doe-eyed,
like he's gonna cry again.

I feel safe with Matt
holding me like this.
He knows how to handle me.

I've been jumping to conclusions,
like Nathan,
and letting my devil
get the better of me.

I take a deep breath in and out again.
I nod for Matt to continue.

"I was gonna say,
          the future
                    may not be
                              too far away."

"What do you mean?" I ask, this time.

"I've been rereading our messages,
especially the ones when I told you
what happened in the lunch hall.
You asked what I said to Kojo.
I felt so ashamed and embarrassed
that I didn't say anything to him.
It got me thinking, and I reckon

it's because I'm used to ignoring
those kinds of comments, you know,
from my parents and at church."

"This isn't news to me," I say.
"You're not the only one
who rereads our messages.
I understand your situation.
Well, I can accept it, at least."

Matt squeezes my leg again.
"I haven't finished," he says.
"I'm ready to come out to The Boys.
Not to my parents yet,
but to The Boys, at least."

I wait, but he's stopped speaking.

"Why now?" I ask.

I watch him weigh his words.
"From how they've been with you,
and how they handled Kojo,
I've got a lot more faith in them."

"So, you come out to The Boys
and then what?" I ask, still processing.

"I come out to The Boys
and then we can be together."
Matt says this like it's obvious.

"We can be together?"
I repeat in the form of a question this time,
mocking Matt's oversimplification.

Matt looks more wounded than me.

I say it again, pointedly.
"You'll come out to The Boys
and then we can be together?
It's as simple as that, is it?
What about everyone else?
What about my mum and Vass?
What about Obi?" I ask.

"Would you really rather be with Obi
if you could be with me?" Matt asks,
with a shocking amount of confidence.

I know this confidence isn't put on.
These are his real feelings showing.

"You've known I was in love with you
this whole time, haven't you?"
I let out a laugh from nowhere.

My anger subsides under the tide
of my irrepressible love for Matt
rushing in and filling my whole body,
even the parts that hurt so badly.

"Of course I know, Kai." He laughs.

I cover my eyes with my right hand.

"We can tell your mum if you want,
and we can tell Vass together today."

"Really?!" I ask, grinning
like I'm a little boy
being told he's getting a puppy
after years of asking for one,
or being told he's going to Disney
and his family is bringing
his best friend with them.

"Best friends to boyfriends," Matt says.
"I've been thinking about it
ever since Nicky Anderson's house party,
and even more since Obi's.
I said 'I'm in love with you' by text message,
but you took it as a joke.
I said 'I love you' to your face once before school.
It's hard to have a serious conversation with you.
We're either joking around
or you're angry about something."

I remember the text: it was a joke.
I remember a winking face emoji.

I remember him saying "I love you" before school.
He was doing his church pastor character
but he said "I love you" in his own voice.

I don't like Matt's description of me

as either joking or angry.
He, of all people, should know
there's more to me than that.

"Why would you want to be boyfriends
if I'm so temperamental?" I ask.

"I can handle you."
Matt winks at me.

I wanna punch him,
but that would prove him right.

I am temperamental.

He can handle me.

I crack   a half smile.
I feel   so exposed.
I feel   vulnerable.
I feel   seen by him.

I wanna agree to be with him.
I wanna be Matt's boyfriend.

Here in Vass's Pride-full bedroom,
Matt and I feel possible,
irrepressible even.

I'm loved, supported,
and endlessly inspired by Vass,
but Vass's bedroom isn't

the world Matt lives in.

Matt believes in something different.
He doesn't live under the evil eye's protection.

Vass's bedroom isn't
our gossipy school.
Vass's bedroom isn't
Matt's church
or homophobic home.

Vass has so much to face
when they step outside each day.
But at least Vass has this bedroom
and a mum who loves and accepts them.
A mum who they can talk to.

I know I could talk to
Theía Estélla as well.
But it's not the same.

I love Vass and Matt differently.

Vass is the best friend
I could ever wish for.

Matt could be the boyfriend
I've always dreamed of.

Best friends to boyfriends
makes sense with Matt.
It's a dream come true.

It's the perfect conclusion
to my coming-out story.

I know I'm far from perfect,
but Matt's in love with me.

Matt is my favorite boy,
and so many people already
thought we were a couple.

The gossip spread by Jyoti.
T asking me about it. The Boys, too.

Vass joking:
        "You're not in love with him, are you?"

Me denying I was in love with Matt,
even though I knew I was.

Joking with Matt and Mum:
        "Absolutely dreamy! Stunning!
        Gorgeous! Tens across the board!"

I wasn't joking, was I?

Matt's all that and more.

I want to obey my heart, but
my mind has other ideas.

Jyoti said it could be a mistake to make
your romantic partner your everything.

It feels too rushed to say yes
to being boyfriends right away.

Matt looks at me expectantly,
and I know what I have to say.

"Thank you for telling me, but
I need time to think about this.
I don't wanna rush
into becoming boyfriends.
I don't wanna risk
losing you as a best friend."

I think of how casually he touches me;
I think of how safe it feels to be touched by him.
I think of how I "come back" to him
when I get upset or angry.
I think of how different things might be
if we were boyfriends, and it fills me with worry.

"I understand," Matt says, smiling
but crestfallen, like Jyoti the other day.

I trust he does understand.
How could he not?

"I still want you to stay for lunch,"
I say, as if that's any consolation.
"Only if you still want to—?" I ask.

He thinks about it for a moment.

"Yeah, I'd like to stay," he says,
"if it's not too awkward for you."

"I can live with awkward,"
I say with another half smile,
as I point to my right arm and leg
on their stacks of cushions.
"What I can't live without is you."

His eyes well up again.
"Can I have another hug?" he asks.

"Yes, of course." I laugh.

I reach out my left arm
and invite Matt back
into my half embrace,
while the flowers from Obi
loom large over us.

MONDAY: MATT'S COMING OUT–
LUNCH HALL

Matt corrals The Boys
with his hushed tone.
"You know I said I wasn't gay
when you asked me?"

"Yeah . . . ," says Nathan, in anticipation.

Kwesi, Abdi, and Sam stay silent.
We all lean closer and wait
for Matt to continue.

"I'm sorry I lied to you.
I am gay," Matt says.
He smiles at me before continuing:
"I don't want my parents to find out,
so I've been trying to keep it quiet."

Quiet is an understatement.
Matt lied to The Boys and Jyoti to keep it secret.

He wasn't ready, my angel reminds me.

"You know what that means?" asks Abdi.

"No, what does it mean?" asks Matt.

"This group is one-third gay," says Abdi.
"That's way above the national average,"
he adds innocently.

The Boys burst into laughter.

I laugh through the pain
of my elbow in its sling.

Even after all
The Boys and I have been through
at lunchtimes
and after school,
the police, the detentions,
me and Matt coming out,
and Nicky Anderson's house party,
it still feels surreal
to be a part of this group,
and even stranger
to realize Abdi
isn't counting Kojo.

It seems Kojo is no longer one of The Boys
because of his homophobic comment.

Even though this is what I wanted

(Matt to come out,
and Kojo extracted from the group like a wobbly tooth),
it doesn't feel like a victory for me.

I'm happy that Matt's
come out to The Boys.

I'm more comfortable
without Kojo at our lunch table.

But I still wish Matt
came out sooner than this.

And I still wish Kojo
hadn't been homophobic.

Nathan has a question:
"So, you're both gay,
but you've never been together?"

Matt looks at me sheepishly,
and I still can't read his mind,
but I know that he'll be fine
with whatever my answer is.

"We've never been together," I say.
I point to my boot and sling.
"Unfortunately, for all interested parties,
my dance card is full.
The doctor said no high-impact activities
for six to eight weeks."

The Boys burst into rapturous laughter.

"What's so funny?" I say, deadpan.
I shrug in my sling.
This makes The Boys laugh harder.

Other kids at nearby lunch tables
turn to look, but none of us care.

"You're so random," chuckles Nathan.

Matt smiles and nods his approval.

Sam leans over to me
with a gentle whisper:
"I think you and Matt
would go good together."

SIDE BY SIDE–IN THE PARK–AFTER SCHOOL

We're side by side
on a bench facing the playground.
Our backpacks rest at Matt's feet.

Matt carried my heavy
backpack for me
all day at school today.

After The Boys at lunchtime,
Matt and I went to find Jyoti,
and he came out to her as well.

We've sworn Jyoti to secrecy.
T is the only person she's allowed
to speak to about me and Matt.

"There they are."
I point at T and Jyoti
as they exit the playground,
each holding a twin by the hand.

As they get closer,
I see T has Olivia
and Jyoti has Sophia.

"Kai!" "Kai!"
The Twins call out to me.

"Wait," T yells
as The Twins pull free
and run toward me.

When they don't stop,
T calls after them: "Remember,
you can't jump on him."

"Okay," The Twins agree in unison
as they race in my direction.

"Get ready to meet my cousins."
I beam at Matt.

"I'm ready!"
Matt beams back.

I feel love rush toward us.
My cousins about to meet
my best friend and crush.

The Twins halt in front of us,
side by side.
"You're Matt!" Olivia says.

"That's right!" Matt laughs.
"Who told you that?"

Olivia points back at T and Jyoti.

T puts an arm around Jyoti
and nuzzles at her neck.

"Matt?" Olivia begins.

"Yes?" Matt responds.

"Do you know our names?" she asks.

"Olivia and Sophia," he says proudly,
as if he's passed an important test.

"Do you know
who is Olivia and
who is Sophia?"
Sophia nudges in,
trying to occupy
the same spot
as her twin sister
in the glow of
Matt's attention
and the golden
afternoon sun.

"I'm sorry, I don't,"
Matt says honestly.
"Will you tell me?"

"I'm Olivia."
Sophia lies convincingly.

"I'm Sophia."
Olivia catches on instantly.

An expert liar himself,
I'm sure Matt knows
that he's being lied to.
I wonder if he considers
playing along with them.

"Is that true?" he asks,
with the gravitas
of Pastor Matthew.

Both girls get the giggles.
They turn to each other
and laugh even harder:
an irrepressible joy bouncing
back and forth between them.

"Was Matt there
when you fell from the wall?"
Olivia asks me.

I turn to Matt.

I recall his helpless face
through the cloud of chalk
thrown up by my impact.

"Yes, he was there," I say.

"Why didn't he catch you?"
Olivia asks me innocently.

T and Jyoti swoop in
and lift The Twins up into the air
before I have a chance to answer.

Olivia and Sophia howl with laughter,
as T and Jyoti throw them up

and

catch them.

I turn and tease Matt:
"Why didn't you catch me?"

Matt laughs at this question
coming from me
and not a five-year-old.

"I'm ready to catch you now,"
Matt says, becoming serious.
"The question is:
Are you ready to fall for me?"

TWO MONTHS LATER: IT'S A WRAP–
NIGHTTIME–MY BEDROOM

"It's so hard!" I say to Matt
as I unravel the long red strip of fabric
and free my hand from the wrap,
which coils like a snake on my lap.

"Come on, Kai. You can do it."

"I can if you help me," I say
as I bat my eyelashes at my boyfriend.

"Let's watch the video again,"
Matt says with the patience of a referee.
He smiles and pats my knee.

I feel a surge of electricity
through my body,
like when I fell from the bouldering wall
onto the crash mat.

The difference being that I fall for this Matt

dozens of times every day,
with every touch and look and word he says.

Matt's shifting weight rocks my mattress
as he leans in
to show me the hand-wrapping video on his phone,
for what feels like the millionth time.

"Why can't you wrap my hands forever?" I sulk.
"It was so romantic when you did it last week.
Even Kojo said so."

"Don't you think he's trying
too hard to show us
he's not homophobic?" Matt asks.
"He always has something
nice to say these days."

"Well, he has no choice
if he wants to be one of The Boys.
Now we're both out
and the rest of them
have made it clear where they stand:
Kojo can either be our ally
or our lonely enemy.
Our gay agenda is well underway.
Mwahahaha!" I evil-villain laugh.

Matt laughs obligingly at me being silly,
the way boyfriends kinda know they have to.

"If it were up to me," Matt says suggestively,

"I'd do it for you forever, but it's not up to me.
TJ said you have to wrap your own hands."

"You just wanna impress TJ," I tease.
"I've never seen you so keen to impress
any other adult the way you try so hard
to impress that man." I roll my eyes playfully.
"Remember, I've seen you on best behavior
around my mum, your parents, and at church,
but with TJ it's on a whole other level."

"I respect him, that's all," Matt says coyly.

"Respect? Is that what we're calling it?" I joke.

"Yes! Because that's all it is!" Matt insists.
"I don't get jealous of The Author's after-school
workshops.
I don't get jealous that you let Vass look at your
notebook."

Vass is the best friend
I could ever wish for.

Matt is the boyfriend
I've always dreamed of.

"You sound a little bit jealous," I joke.
I make a pinching gesture
with my thumb and index finger
in front of my face.

Obi's face flashes in my memory.
I need to leave Obi in the past.

"I'm not jealous." Matt laughs nervously.

I force myself into the present
and then beyond into the future.

"You can read something at the end of term," I say.
"The Author's helping us make our own anthology.
Everyone from the workshops
has to put in at least one piece.
The Author's our editor and Jyoti's his assistant.
It's gonna be a proper book with an ISBN.
It's gonna be cataloged in the British Library."

"Swear down?!" Matt exclaims
in unexpected recognition.
"The big red building
between King's Cross and Euston?
Statue of Isaac Newton out front?"

"I'm not sure," I admit.
"I've not been there before.
Have you been there?"

"Yeah!" Matt beams at me.
"I went with my parents to an exhibition
about Malorie Blackman."

I feel a pang of jealousy
that Matt did this without me.

That Matt went with his parents.

That Mum didn't make time
to take me when I asked.

I don't understand why Matt
hasn't mentioned it until now.

Matt knows
I love Malorie's books,
especially *Noughts & Crosses.*

I'm not cross with Matt.
If anything, I'm impressed
he took an interest
in an author I love.

Is that what happened?
Or did his parents force him to go?

Before I have a chance to ask him,
Matt says: "I'm proud of you, Kai.
You're gonna be an author
and one day you'll have published
over seventy books like Malorie Blackman
and there'll be an exhibition all about you."

"Yeah, one day," I say hopefully.

I imagine seventy books.

My name on their spines.

I imagine an exhibition.

My sky-blue notebook.

Books that inspire me.

Skellig by David Almond.

Noughts & Crosses by Malorie.

What a goal to aim for.

What a future to hope for.

I feel tearful, in the best possible way.

Matt sees a bright future ahead of me.

All of a sudden,
I'm in the past again
with no control
of my overthinking.

"What's wrong, Kai?"

"Obi definitely stopped
coming to youth squad
because of me." I sigh.
"He must really hate me!"
I say melodramatically,
with the back of my hand
lifted to my forehead,

to play it off as a joke,
even though
       I'm deadass.
       I'm serious.

I'm that boy: Malachi,
           the overthinker,
who can't think straight
           under pressure
and has a problem with anger.

"How could anyone hate you?"
Matt takes my hand down
and gives it a gentle squeeze.
"Spider Girl said Obi's brother
moved their band practice
from Sunday to Saturday.
Why won't you believe that?"

"Because it's obviously not true.
I just thought we could all
stay friends," I say weakly.
"Obi replies when I text him,
but he never texts me first.
It's not that I feel sorry for him,
but when I remember
certain things he told me,
he seemed like
he needed more friends."

"You were never friends
with Obi to begin with," Matt says.

"I don't see any problem
with Obi's behavior at the moment.
You're begging it with him now
because you feel bad for how it ended.
Obi doesn't wanna be friends
with you, or with any of us."

"That's a bit harsh," I reply.

Matt puts a hand on my knee.
"You can disagree with me,
but here's how I see it:
Obi only invited me and Vass
to his house to be polite,
and to get us on side,
but ultimately to get you
into his bedroom.
I don't know, Kai.
At least Obi didn't ghost you
after you told him
you didn't wanna keep seeing him.
He still replies to your texts.
Give him a break.
Maybe you'll be friends one day.
But maybe right now he's upset.
Maybe he's too polite to ask you
to leave him alone."

As I let Matt's words sink in,
I find I don't disagree with him.

I try to imagine a mirror world,

with double dates and band lyrics,
where I'm boyfriends with Obi,
and still best friends with Matt.

Would Matt be giving me advice
about my relationship with Obi?

Now that I'm boyfriends with Matt,
there's no other world
or universe that matters to me.

I know I have to let Obi go.
I know I have a future with Matt
            and no future with Obi.

"You're so insightful," I tell him.
Followed by, "And beautiful."
Followed by, "I love you."

"I love you, too," Matt says.
"And I love your mum
for letting me sleep over so often."

"She seems to think
you're a good influence on me," I say.
"Whatever could've given her that idea?"
I ask sarcastically, hinting
at Matt's Church Boy act around Mum.

I don't think Matt gets that I'm joking.
He gives serious thought
to my rhetorical question.

"Your mum's cool, you know."

Matt says this as if cool means something else.
As if cool means hope for his future.
As if cool means a possibility of his family
accepting him the way my mum has.
As if cool means permission to be his full self.

"Yes, I guess she is kinda cool," I admit.
"Although I asked her to take me
to that exhibition at the British Library
but she wouldn't take a day off work."

"Kai, do you know why you get so angry
about not spending more time with your mum?"
Matt asks, before answering his own question:
"It's because you actually enjoy her company.
I hate spending time with my parents.
I can't be my real self around them.
Even at that exhibition they were so strict
about the way I had to look at it.
They forced me to look at every case,
read every caption, and watch every video in order.
When I just wanted to move freely around the space
and look at whatever took my interest.
I know that sounds like a minor thing
but when you deep it,
everything's like that with my parents.
They make things that could be fun feel like a chore.
I remember thinking, 'I wish I was here with Kai.'
But I didn't want you to have to suffer my parents.

I thought of suggesting the two of us went together
but my parents ask so many questions
when I wanna go into central London without them."
Matt stops and smirks at me.
"Maybe they worry I'll go to Soho
now I look old enough to get into a bar.
A part of me thinks
my parents already know I'm gay,
but I'm not gonna confirm it to them unless
they ask me or I've moved out for uni,
whichever comes first.
But being out to your mum,
Vass, The Boys, Jyoti, and T,
I feel, I don't know, a glimmer
of what it might feel like in the future
to be fully out to everyone.
Do you get what I'm saying, Kai?
Your mum is like a ray of light—in my life, at least."

"I get you," I say, and I do.

What Theía Estélla is to me
is what my mum is to Matt.

I try to explain this to him:
"I think we look elsewhere
for what our parents can't give us.
Vass's mum is that ray of light for me.
That's one of the things I've been discussing
with the school counselor:
how it takes a village to raise a child.
I guess my mum's part of your village now."

Matt's eyes go glassy,
he looks tearful,
but he doesn't let his tears flow.
He sniffs
and shakes his head,
and when he replies it's not what I expect.

"Who gives the best advice," he asks,
"me or the school counselor?"

"You," I say,
and it's true.
I grin at him.
"You give the best everything."

Matt smiles back at me:
I'm confident
he catches my meaning.

We're not virgins anymore.

With one end in each hand,
I grasp the long red strip of fabric and toss it,
making a loop around
his broad back and shoulders.
My arms complete the loop.

With one end in each hand,
I use the fabric to pull Matt toward me.

We're nose to nose,

almost kissing, like
boxers at a weigh-in.

Matt leans back and the loop becomes taut.

"You're not getting
another kiss from me
until you can wrap
your hands properly."

I release my grip
on both ends of the fabric,
and expect Matt to fall
backward onto the bed.

"Nice try, Malachi!"
He holds a mid-sit-up position
with such confidence and ease.

I shake my head and roll my eyes.
"Stop showing off!"

"You love it!" Matt flexes his biceps,
still holding himself in a mid-sit-up.

I rest my hands on his chest
and gently push him backward.

Matt wraps his arms around me
in a full and strong embrace.
I let myself fall forward
as he falls back onto my bed.

I rest on top of Matt
like I'm the Sphinx,
and he is my limestone bedrock.
He lies there in surrender to me,
a cat that's caught his prey.

Matt smiles as he looks up.
"What are you thinking, my little devil?"

"Wanna have sex?"
I ask him, half joking, half hoping.

I'm rocked by the vibration of
his howling laughter,
an earthquake of joy.

"No more procrastination . . ." He toys with me.

Without breaking eye contact,
Matt retrieves the long red strip of fabric
from behind his back and hands it to me.

He knows how to handle me.

"It's your turn to be on
best behavior," he says.

I bite my lip, turned on
by his firm tone.

Matt slowly shakes his head

and changes character.

"Malachi Michaelides," Pastor Matthew begins,
"it's my mission to teach you
self-control and discipline.
No sex, not even one kiss,
until you've mastered this."

It's cute how Matt thinks he's in charge
when I have him where
I've always wanted him.

When Matt acts like a Big Man,
I get to play at being his little devil.

ACKNOWLEDGMENTS

Editor – Alexandra Cooper
Production Editor – Erin DeSalvatore
Designer – Jenna Stempel-Lobell
Production Manager – Vanessa Nuttry
Marketing & Publicity – Michael D'Angelo, John Sellers
Copyeditor – Jessica White
Proofreader – Dan Janeck

Thank you to Metal Culture for sponsoring my artist residency at Studio 459 in Tomar, Portugal, where I completed a draft of this book, and to Mark and Joao at Studio 459 for your hospitality.